# Roots

## of

# Deceit

## The Miss Hyde Collection II

# Kindra

# Sowder

ROOTS OF DECEIT   Kindra Sowder

This Edition published by Kindra Sowder Media, an imprint of ELK Publications, in 2022 in the United States of America

ISBN: 978-1-947584-83-9

Copyright © Kindra Sowder 2015, 2020, 2022

Cover art by WJR Parks, 2022

Edited by Edd Sowder, 2017, 2020, 2022

Format by ELK Publications, 2022

# CONTENTS

## AFTER  MIDNIGHT

## MISCREANT

# ROOTS OF DECEIT   Kindra Sowder

# AFTER MIDNIGHT

## CHAPTER ONE

I had always wondered how my family had come to earn the affliction of the murderous, dark half. So, it shouldn't have surprised me that somehow, somewhere, a stranger held the very answers in his hands in the form of old journals and drawings. I also should have always known that there were more out there like myself.

After all, Hyde had to come from somewhere, right?

A part of me lived with a blindfold on for all these years, completely ignorant to what I was. I still didn't know enough about my lineage, or my condition for that matter, to be confident enough to come out and say the words. At some point, I knew I would need to come to terms with it. I took all sexuality from a man, killed him, and took what was most important to him as my own.

His heart.

Just knowing that Hyde wasn't interested in anything Emmett had to offer was beyond me. She had

1

been like that from the first moment I met him—quiet and lingering just underneath the surface. Nothing like she was with other men. Especially Johan and Mitch after their kidnap and torture session. She tore them apart easily enough, as if they were pieces of tissue paper. It awed and disgusted me all at once, seeing my own hands rip into flesh—covered in blood and gore just like she did with so many others. But not Emmett, which created more questions than answers.

Was there a particular trigger? Was there something inside these other men that caused her to unleash all that rage?

I guessed it didn't matter now, since we had come to a truce of sorts.

Either way—whether it mattered or not—I sat in my bedroom, perched on my bed in my plush bathrobe, flipping through some of the documents Cyra left courtesy of Adam Burnside. My wet hair dripped, small rivulets of cool water running down my skin and soaking into my robe.

I was supposed to be getting ready for a dinner date with Emmett but had been easily distracted by the documents and the massive journal beckoning to me from the desk in my bedroom I hardly ever used. The first ancestor to peek at me from between the pages had been killed during the Salem Witch Trials—murdered for the affliction she couldn't help. It made me wonder who else had fallen as a result.

Pushing past those pages detailing her final moments, I came across a page that showed a brilliant, green, and slightly glowing piece of jewelry posed on the page alongside something that looked a lot like an old statue. Before I could focus on the page, my cell phone buzzed beside the book, pulling my attention. The sound came from nowhere, nearly causing me to jump out of my skin and my heart to leap from within my throat.

"Jesus Christ," I shouted, reaching forward, and taking the vibrating phone in my palm. Not even taking a look at the caller I.D., I swiped the green button on the touch screen and placed it to my ear. "Hello?"

"Jeez, Blythe. From the sound of your voice, I'd swear you were going to the gallows than on a date with one of the hottest men to roam the Earth," Lauren's voice screeched through the speaker.

"Oh, stop it," I chided.

"So, he going to get lucky tonight?" she asked.

Tilting my head to the side, I held the phone between my ear and shoulder to free up both hands to gather the papers and the journal up to put them away.

3

"Lauren, can I ask you a question?" I asked, stuffing the loose pages in the massive book, and thumping the cover closed.

"Sure thing. What's up?" Her voice lilted at the end as if she were genuinely curious in what I was about to ask.

"Do you think with anything else except your vagina?"

Her shrill laughter pierced my ear drum as I stood up and crossed the room to set everything on my dresser, pulling open a drawer to find a bra and panties to wear. I wanted something nice, but not too slutty. I had already slept with him, and according to some, the date would be the next logical step. Most would argue it was supposed to be the other way around, but they didn't have a murderous alter ego to worry about either. The psychological trauma of what Mitch and Johan did still lingered fresh in my mind, but in the quest of solidity between the two of us, Hyde seemed to have taken that pain from me so I could move past it for something I genuinely wanted. Hyde and I had bonded, coming to an agreement. I get what I want, she gets what she wants. Simple and easy.

So far.

Lauren's voice dropped to a deep sultry tone as she replied, "Only on occasion."

I rolled my eyes.

"Of course."

"What are your plans?" Lauren laughed in my ear.

"Well, I know we're going out to dinner, but that's about it. I let him take the reins on this one," I replied, quickly discarding the robe, and slipping into a pair of black, lace panties and matching bra.

"That's not like you," Lauren nearly gasped. "Does he give good head? Is that why you're letting him decide?"

I moved into the bathroom, coming to stand in front of the sink, catching my reflection in the mirror. My hair was starting to curl because I had let it go so long without blow drying it. I raked my fingers through it and glared at the defiant curls that had formed, reaching for the blow dryer, and plugging it into the outlet by the mirror.

*Keep it. Emmett may like it*, Hyde voiced in my head.

When my eyes met my reflection, it was almost as if Lauren and the phone didn't exist. Both eyes were bleeding green, spreading outward from my pupil like writhing snakes. Leaning forward, I reached up with one finger and pulled down the bottom lid of my left eye, swallowing hard at the sight. I took a deep, steadying breath as my heart began to race, and closed my eyes.

"We had a deal," I whispered.

"What? I'm sorry, I couldn't hear you," Lauren asked, snapping me out of my fugue.

Shaking my head and opening my eyes, I answered, "It's nothing. Don't worry about it."

The line was quiet for all of a moment, and then she took a deep breath as if she knew I was hiding something and was frustrated by that fact.

"Yeah? You sure? If not, you can always ditch Emmett and we can have a night in," she suggested.

I shook my head, forgetting that she couldn't see me do it.

"No, no, I'm fine. Maybe tomorrow night?"

"Sure, sounds good," she responded.

My phone buzzed against my ear before I had a chance to say anything else, startling me again. Emmett's name flashed across the screen as the device vibrated against my palm, and a smile instantly spread over my lips, calming my anxiousness immediately.

Placing the phone back against my ear, I said, "Hey, Lauren, it's Emmett on the other line. I've got to go, but we'll talk tomorrow, okay?"

"Don't do anything I wouldn't do," she teased.

Of course, there wasn't anything she wouldn't do, but her point was clear enough.

"And be careful out there. That sick fuck killed another woman the other day."

"I will. Promise."

"You better."

Without saying another word, I switched to the other line, the grin on my face instant. I felt Hyde stir warm in my belly but pushed her down as best I could. Yes, we had a deal and she behaved most of the time, but when my mind went to Emmett she stirred. When I was in his presence, she was practically silent, which opened up a lot of other questions I was too afraid to ask.

My reflection's expression changed, the genuine smile turning into a sadistic smirk that curled up at the corners with evil. I turned quickly away from it, the sight making me breathless, turning toward the hallway that led out into the living room. The warm flutter in my chest picked up, and then quieted only to pick up again as I cleared my throat, preparing to speak. I walked back into the bedroom and re-acquired the robe haphazardly thrown on the chair beside the door. I wrapped it around me, allowing it to remain untied to where the chilled air in the room could caress my skin.

"You're late," I scolded.

"I know, babe, but I'm close," Emmett replied.

"Oh, you are, huh?" I felt the smile grow wider before I could stop it as I walked into the living room.

"Yup."

"Where are you?"

There was a knock on the door leading out of the apartment, and my heart skipped a beat. My entire body warmed up, my skin feeling as if a thousand fireworks had gone off under the surface. I stopped in my tracks and ran my free hand through my still slightly wet hair.

"Open the door, baby," he crooned into the phone.

I could barely hear him through the solid dark wood of the door, but even though it was extremely muted, I could still tell it was him on the other side. It took my body less than half a second to move toward it, reaching out and turning the knob to greet him. In his presence, my body almost acted on its own without much thought. Of course, with Hyde taking a backseat when it came to my want for a relationship with a man, I didn't have to be scared of what she'd do anymore. Dax was still in my mind at times, but I found I could somehow move on. Not like I knew him well enough to be truly hung up on his death, and my hands being the ones to deal it was punishment enough. I didn't have to shoulder the guilt anymore, just like I didn't have to hold onto the fear of what Johan and Mitch did either.

She did that for me.

She locked it all away in some deep, dark corner that not even I could find. That didn't bother me. It could all stay there as far as I was concerned.

The door swung open and the knob slipped from my fingers, knocking softly against the wall. Emmett stood on the other side, phone still held up to his ear, and as beautiful as ever. His brown eyes were sultry, hair messy but not in such a way it looked awful. His leather jacket hugged him in all the right places, white V-neck t-shirt snug across his pecs. Perfect as always with fingertips tinged lightly with different colors he used in his paintings.

I put my phone down at my side, and then slid it into the pocket of my robe, Emmett mirroring my movements as he tucked his away in his jacket pocket. That happened sometimes. We moved as one without

9

even realizing it, causing Hyde to react for reasons I didn't know or understand, and wasn't certain that I wanted to. My breathing picked up and my heart slammed against my ribcage, a soft sheen of sweat breaking out over my flesh. The room grew far too hot.

"Hey," he grinned, taking a step through the threshold.

I took a step backward and smiled in return. He closed the door behind him, eyes moving up and down my body, obviously noticing the robe.

"You're not ready?" he asked, his brow furrowing for all of a second before smoothing out.

"Not yet," I answered, turning away, and removing the robe as I moved back toward my bedroom, "but it won't take me long to finish up. I just have to slip into something a little less," I turned my head and met his gaze, making certain my hips rolled to draw his eyes, "revealing."

Turning back around, I walked down the hallway, into my room, and to the closet—Emmett's footsteps following close behind. Moving through my walk-in closet, my fingertips grazed each piece of fabric on the hangers like lost lovers until I stopped at one that I knew I just had to wear. Removing it from the rack, I held it out in front of me and rubbed the soft, crimson cotton between my fingers. The dress, once on, would reach just below my knees, three-quarter sleeves would battle the slight chill in the air as winter made its way into New York.

"Blythe," I heard him say my name from beyond the doorway.

Glancing up and then back to the dress in my hands, I asked, "Yeah?"

"We have reservations in twenty minutes. We've got to get going if we want to make it in time."

"I know."

I slipped the dress off the hanger and then over my head, slipping softly over my skin in an almost seductive way. After a second of searching, I found a pair of black ankle boots and a leather jacket that looked a lot like the one Emmett was wearing. Letting my hair air-dry, I ran my fingers through it and turned to him with a bright smile that I made certain reached my eyes.

"All right, let's go," I breathed, stepping out from within the closet while slipping my purse onto my shoulder. Going without makeup to dinner would normally be a sin in some circles but with my complexion—plus Hyde making me seem more seductive anyway. I really didn't need any.

It was the first moment I truly noticed him since he entered my apartment, and my breath caught in my throat as buzzing heat resonated throughout my core. Swallowing hard, I let his deep browns take me in, approving as he smirked, and his eyes lit up with desire that flashed through them like a wildfire. He stepped into me, my breasts grazing his chest as heat ignited between us. He bit his lip with a hooded gaze, massive hands grabbing my hips and pulling me closer. Staring at him, I realized his jaw was lined with a shadow of stubble. It was sexy as Hell, and I breathed him in. He smelled slightly of paint thinner, but it was covered up by the smell of him. That musky, masculine scent that made my head swim and my stomach ache. Leaning down, he placed his head next to mine, that same stubble brushing my temple deliciously while he took a deep breath in, as if memorizing my scent as well.

"Or maybe we can miss it," he sang softly, his breath hot against my ear as his breathing picked up.

Placing my palm against the center of his chest, I felt his heart race just underneath—fluttering with anticipation like it had that first time. Then there it was again. Fire swept through me and reached up into my eyes, but I pulled it back. She was hungry, but now wasn't the time. We had a deal, and I wasn't about to let her go back on it.

"No, let's still go." I turned my face to the side do that my lips brushed his ear, whispering the next words into it. "I'm famished."

# CHAPTER TWO

I took a small sip of my whiskey sour as the waiter placed my rare, bloodied steak in front of me. The acrid liquid burned its way down my throat, warming me from the inside out, working to silence Hyde's presence so that maybe Emmett and I could talk in peace. No matter what I may have thought prior about relationships, I did genuinely like him and did want to know more. As far as I could tell, he was an open book. It was just up to me to actually read what the pages inside offered.

He sat there, quietly watching as I considered him thoughtfully. His lips perked up at one corner in a smile. The food before him, a salad of all things, offered no other information than his healthy eating habits. Anything we did up to that point, which took place in my bedroom or his, only spoke of attentiveness and a touch of promiscuity. I could always read more into that attentive behavior in the bedroom if I wanted to take a note or two from Freud, but I wanted nothing to do with the fact that it could have to do with his mother. That was a rabbit hole I wasn't about to go down, no matter how alluring the man was.

# ROOTS OF DECEIT  Kindra Sowder

Ignorance is bliss, and I was perfectly content for it to stay that way as far as that went.

Everything else. I wanted to know everything else. Maybe, if given the chance to get to truly know him, Hyde would back off and decide he had no place in her horrid games.

"Thank you," Emmett said to the server as she set down another beer—a very dark lager—in front of him. I could smell the hops from across the table.

She practically beamed as her eyes roamed over him when she answered, "You're welcome, sir."

Her voice was high-pitched—annoying—and seeped with the urge to please. I knew it was intended for him. That much was clear in her demeanor, especially when she didn't even look at me to see if I needed anything else. After all, my drink was already down to the last sip.

"I'll have another whiskey sour," I said, tipping my glass so the ice clinked together.

Looking up my eyes locked with the server's sky-blue ones just long enough for her tanned skin to turn pale when she saw something in mine. Hyde, no doubt, made her presence known in some way, causing the girl to quickly turn on her heels and walk toward the bar without saying a word. All I felt was the heat from the whiskey slither through my body. That could have been a mixture of her and the alcohol, but there was no way to tell.

"So," I began, sitting my now empty tumbler on the hard wood table with a *clink*, "where did you grow up? Were you close to your parents?"

The question sounded awkward as soon as it left my mouth. I wasn't particularly good at small talk outside the gallery where it was necessary to close deals sometimes. But here, I could sense he picked up on how obviously nervous it made me when his smile grew until I thought he would laugh.

"Well, we moved around a lot," he answered, lifting the glass of beer to his lips to take a long sip. When he set it down, he licked his lips and took a deep breath, still smiling. "Blythe, we don't have to do the weird small talk bullshit. I'd like for this to just happen naturally, and for us to get to know one another," he reached forward and run his fingertips softly over my knuckles, "organically."

The sensation caused my body to instantly warm. Swallowing, I leaned forward and placed my hand over his.

With a soft, sensual smile, I replied, "I'd like that."

"I thought you would."

He smirked, and Hyde went silent inside and more importantly, in my head. The server sauntered back over with my drink, setting it down on the table and snatching her hand back like I'd bite her.

"Can I get you two anything else?" she quipped, ringing her hands in front of her.

"No, we're fine. Thank you," Emmett interjected as soon as I opened my mouth, never breaking eye contact with me.

I heard her muted steps when she walked away, muttering something unintelligible under her breath as she did so. The soft glow of the lights played with the color of Emmett's dark eyes, making them seem sultry, filled with ravishing heat.

"Anyway, to finish answering your question, I wasn't close to my parents. They've been gone for a while now, but I can't say I miss them. It would be a lie."

Sitting back, gently removing his hand from mine, he picked up his fork and stabbed the lightly dressed greens of his salad. I cleared my throat and made an honest attempt at my steak, cutting through it before spearing a bite-sized piece of the rare meat with the silver tines of my fork. I placed it in my mouth and chewed. It exploded with the slight taste of iron and the flavor of the meat.

"That's a shame," I comforted as I chewed.

"What about you?" Emmett asked, gaze piercing as he stuffed a bite of salad into his mouth, a bright red cherry tomato visible past the green.

"I've always lived in New York. To be honest, I don't think I'd ever leave. I love it here. It's the only place I have ever known to have something to do at any time of the day or night," I answered, hoping he'd let me skip the bit about my parents entirely.

"And your parents?"

I cringed, and quickly reconfigured my facial expression before I answered, taking another bite of my steak. I couldn't look at him—could barely look up and away from my plate.

"They died when I was seventeen," I responded swiftly, letting the words fall out into an uncomfortable heap on the table between us.

"Oh," I heard the interest in his voice. "If you don't mind me asking, how did they pass?"

A morbid question, but could I answer it? The sensible, guarded part of me didn't want to, but the rash, earnest part of me did just to see what his reaction would be. Then the question was, did I go with the lie I was told my entire life, or did I go with the truth? Well, half of the truth.

The words left my mouth before I had a chance to stop them.

"They were murdered," I spat out.

I cleared my throat and continued to look down, placing my knife and fork on the plate. That was when I noticed the lack of sounds coming from Emmett's side of the table. When I looked up, he sat there frozen to the spot—dark eyes wide, face pale with fork poised over his food.

"Um, I'm sorry. I didn't mean to just say it like that," I almost stammered. "I wasn't thinking."

He shook his head. "No, it's okay. So were mine."

"Oh," I muttered. "I'm sorry."

Why was I apologizing? He had asked, right? He did, that much was true. Then why did I feel like crawling under the table to never come out again? Granted, Hyde evidently pushed the answer I wasn't even certain I wanted to give right out from between my lips, but should I feel that guilty about it?

Heat rose into my cheeks as a flush moved through my entire body, making me sweat slightly as nerves took over and my heart hammered.

"It's really okay," he insisted.

Those words didn't stop that fact that I was mortified and vulnerable.

"Here I was thinking we wouldn't have anything in common," I joked, laughing softly in an attempt to brush off how the admission made me feel.

"Blythe," he placed his fork down on his napkin beside his plate, "it's really okay. It happened a long time ago. Hell, I barely even remember them, but I can tell you really loved your parents. If you want to talk about it, we can."

I waved my hand in a dismissive gesture, "No, I'd rather not ruin the evening more than I already have."

His face fell. "You didn't ruin anything, Blythe. Look," he adjusted in his seat, making certain to touch my hand with both of his, "we all have a past. It's not always pretty, but it's what makes you, well . . . you, and I really like you a lot, so I'm willing to take on anything you throw at me. Like I said before. You were very up front about who you are, and I'm perfectly fine with whatever comes with that. As long as it's honest and it's you, nothing else matters."

"I know," I said, smiling softly.

"Plus, now you know mine wasn't all sunshine and roses either. We're both broken." He took my hand up, brushing his lips across my knuckles. "Besides, I'm looking forward to putting you back together." There was a slight drawl in his words as he spoke that I had never noticed before.

"Is that Southern charm I sense, Mr. Adler?" I asked, genuine glee taking place of the fear he'd run at the first opportunity.

His face fell.

"North Carolina, born and raised. I hide it well, don't I?" he chuckled.

"Barely. I can catch that Southern drawl around the edges of your words." I grinned wide and picked up my glass, the ice clinking inside the amber liquid of the whiskey. "You've been hiding that all this time?"

"Yeah, well, us Southern boys don't really do too well around here so the choice was kind of made for me."

"And what makes you say that?"

His eyes still held their warmth, but there was a slight tinge of sadness and knowing in them that told of years upon years of a type of wisdom you could only gain through a hard life.

"Experience."

He took a massive gulp of his beer, demolishing at least half of it in one swallow. Taking a dainty sip of my drink, I leaned forward and placed my elbows on the table while holding the cool glass against the side of my neck. One cool drop of condensation rolled down the length of my throat, down toward the V-neck of my dress. It drew his eye, but he quickly snapped his gaze back up to my face—obviously attempting to be a gentleman, which I greatly appreciated even though the heat sparkling in his gaze was the desired reaction.

"Do you want to talk about it?" I asked, genuinely interested.

It hadn't been about only his body since the first time I met him, but it certainly helped things along when it came down to it. The sex—mind-blowing as it was—had been the icebreaker we needed. Hyde agreeing to back off so I could have this made all the difference. If she hadn't, she would have killed him by now. Not that she didn't want to under the surface—I could feel her writhing now when she used to be silent while she tried to figure him out. Something in him had thrown her off, and I felt it too, but it was just at the fringes of my awareness just like she was.

He lifted the glass again to polish off the beer, his entire demeanor changing as I watched. His lips were now set in a grim line with clenched jaw, eyes flicking around in almost a paranoid state, and his neck flushed blazing red that I knew disappeared to the flesh underneath his shirt.

"Not really," he replied through gritted teeth.

My eyes squinted at him, as if doing so could help me see something I missed. Was he bipolar? Was something wrong? His attitude changed as quickly as a flash of lightning, and I wasn't sure if it was something I had done, or something else entirely.

Leaning forward, his stare moved to my plate, steak barely touched while the asparagus and garlic mashed potatoes hadn't been touched at all.

"Can I?" he asked, pointing to my plate.

Confused, I hesitated, looking down at the plate. Red pooled on white, bleeding into the potatoes— turning them slightly pinkish in color. Suddenly, I lost my appetite. After a beat, I realized just what he was asking of me. Nodding, I pushed the plate toward him and took another draw of my near empty glass tumbler of whiskey. The ice clattered against my lips as I did.

"Sure, no problem."

Practically ravenous, he pulled the plate toward him and dug in with the ferociousness of a wild animal that hadn't eaten in weeks. Before I knew it, the steak was gone, and the rest of the meal remained untouched just like a moment before.

# ROOTS OF DECEIT  KINDRA SOWDER

Something was definitely off. I just couldn't tell what, but when his eyes met mine the thought nearly vanished, sitting just on the fringes where Hyde waited. Radiant heat smoldered in his deep brown eyes as well as his expression—yearning mingling with passion, but obviously battling something else within.

Sitting back, barely satiated, he draped his arm over the back of the booth he sat on and grinned, bright white teeth gleaming under the soft lights. Hyde rolled warmly in my belly, branching out in spiderwebs along my nerves. I pushed her down, but she was reacting to something—the same thing I was reacting to as I felt desire unfurl with her. Instead of doing anything about it—joining him on the other side of the booth for a little bit of under-the-table action—I sat and continued to sip my drink, letting the whiskey go to work as it relaxed my shoulders almost painfully.

"You okay?" I asked

"Yeah," he responded, strained, "didn't realize I wanted a steak, is all."

I laughed a little, wondering why he hadn't just ordered his own, but decided against saying it aloud.

"Okay," I chuckled, taking a piece of asparagus between my fingers, placing the tip into my mouth—playing with it a little before taking a bite.

It was mildly flavored, the olive oil and salt on it mixing beautifully with the green flavor of it. His eyes never left my face, the pulse in his neck jackhammering away as I watched. If I hadn't known better, I would have sworn he growled a little.

He wanted more than just the steak, but he was holding back.

Before I could open my mouth to speak, he reached into his jacket pocket and pulled out his cell phone, glancing at the screen. Funny, I hadn't heard it go off.

"Sorry, I have to go," he said in a rushed, snarling tone.

Something in his eyes and his expression was extremely wrong. He refused to look at me, keeping his eyes hooded as he looked down at the floor, with jaw clenched and shoulders squared. A predator ready to pounce.

The thought set me on edge, each hair on the back of my neck standing on end. I just wish I understood why.

In one swift motion, he placed three one-hundred-dollar bills on the table, stood, brushed my lips chastely with his, and began to leave.

"I'll see you later, okay? Do you mind if I come by? Tomorrow?" he asked, scrubbing his stubbled jaw with his palm.

"Uhh . . . sure. I have the day off, so I'll be free all day. You want to—" I was about to see if he wanted to get lunch, but he was gone in a flash, leaving me sitting there with my whiskey in my hand and misunderstanding in my mind.

The only company I had now was confusion, and Hyde . . . and now, she was hungry.

# ROOTS OF DECEIT    Kindra Sowder

# CHAPTER THREE

Hyde's warmth moved throughout my body as soon as he was out of sight, and it didn't take long before I swallowed the remainder of the whiskey in my glass, rose to my feet, and rushed to the restroom, which I hoped was empty. My eyes burned, signaling the changes I attempted to hold back.

I knew how this would go. I would fight it, and end up giving in. She would get what she wanted, even if I didn't always get what I wanted.

Tit for tat. I got a date, no matter how short and awkward, so she got a murder spree.

Pushing through the dark, solid wood door, I was met with at least three more images of myself reflected back at me. Mirrors lined the long wall spaced out to sit in front of each sink. The warm walls were a stunning shade of rusty brown, each handle and stall—anything metal—was brushed copper.

The most stunning sight were my many reflections staring back at me, wide-eyed with irises that shifted from the deep brown I normally had to the bright green Hyde always exhibited when the change took over. My heart beat against my sternum like a sledgehammer, each beat causing another small bead of sweat to roll down my back. I couldn't tell if it was from the alcohol or the change—or both. A chill ran up and down my spine, and I wiped my clammy palms on my dress.

Each stall was empty and not a single person was in sight.

"Thank God," I exclaimed, turning around to see if there was a lock on the entrance door.

There was.

I turned the brushed cooper lock, and heard the faint click. I was finally alone and had some semblance of privacy while she took over. It didn't matter how much I fought it. She typically won. The only times she didn't anymore were the times we agreed it was best for her to remain buried in the deep recesses of my brain. This wouldn't be one of those times. Technically, it was her time, and I would stick to our deal no matter how much I loathed it.

She slithered through me—mind, body, and soul—devouring every piece of me so I'd only hover in the background. Able to see and think, but not able to affect anything. She would be in complete control. I'd be a silent observer much like she was when I was in control.

# ROOTS OF DECEIT KINDRA SOWDER

A tingling sensation wormed its way up my spine and into my skull, out into my fingertips and my toes as I watched the subtle shift of my transformation, leaning against the countertop with palms slick and clammy against the granite. My eyes flickered from brown to green—back and forth until it settled on green, tingling turning into prickling, stinging needle pricks of stunning heat. My cheeks flushed slightly along with my chest and neck. But it quickly disappeared as I felt my own consciousness being pushed into the background, drowned out by Hyde's radiant violent energy. My vision became fuzzy black around the edges, like velvet I could reach out and touch, but couldn't feel. My senses dulled, muffled to the point of feeling like I was touching, seeing, tasting, and hearing everything through a thin film of plastic.

After a few moments, the transformation was complete, and I watched as Hyde pushed away from the counter and quaffed her—my—hair while pouting her lips, using one fingertip to touch up the edges of lipstick.

The fear that used to come to me was long-forgotten, our deal dampening it to the briefest of anxiety at the prospect of having no control over my own body. I didn't have to be afraid of her anymore, even though there was the tiniest part of me that was because of what she stood for. The dark, evil part of me that couldn't move past the existence of evil in others. That was what I attributed her immmergence to. From what I could tell, she could sense something in the men she killed—even Dax, whom I had liked—but what exactly?

Of course, she never wanted to provide an answer. Not up to this point. But maybe one day she would. Maybe I just needed to be patient long enough or find the right way to ask.

Placing her palms against our body, she smoothed down the red dress and primped until she felt we were presentable again. With a heavy sigh, she ran fingers through her hair one more time, took a step away from the mirror, and regarded our appearance once again with scrutiny.

"Much better," she practically growled, my usual tone now deep, seductive, and titillating. "Now, let's go find us a screamer."

If I could have outwardly cringed, I would have. Nonetheless, she walked to the locked door, unperturbed—turned the lock and swung the door open to walk out gracefully. In a flash of movement, she grabbed my small clutch purse, made certain to leave the cash open on the table so the server could see it, and left. Then, before I knew it, we stood in the middle of a club. Techno music played and lights flashed, blazing bright colors against the walls and the bodies moving to the beat against one another.

The music had obviously been remixed from something heavy—rock mostly likely—with deeper, growling vocals that screeched at the appropriate moments. I felt uneasy, but Hyde's rolling emotions of hunger and intrigue easily drowned me out as her eyes scanned the writhing crowd.

The lights and sound waves ran seductively over the moving bodies in perfect rhythm, changing from blues, to red, to purple, ending in red again. There were no strobe lights, just flashing lasers that penetrated a soft fog that rolled through the mass of people. I felt the beat of the music pulse through my body as Hyde began to move with it, swiveling her hips in perfect cadence with it. She started slowly, but then picked up the pace as her feet took us out onto the dance floor, eyes catching those of a man standing at the bar watching the crowd.

After our shared eyes met his, he was hooked and couldn't look away.

# ROOTS OF DECEIT  Kindra Sowder

I couldn't tell what color his eyes were through the haze of seeing through another conscious entity inside me, or past the color of the lights, but I could tell his hair was lighter. Possibly blonde, but I couldn't tell for certain. And his eyes were light, almost white, as they reflected the lasers. A beer bottle grasped in his hand, he clenched his strong jaw, but his full bottom lip, and slipped his free hand into his jeans pocket as he leaned nonchalantly against the bar top. He definitely wasn't her typical target, but I could see why he caught her eye. He was a beautiful man, and there was an edge to him that I sensed through her perceptions. Something I may not have caught otherwise, which almost made me understand how she chose her targets a little bit better.

Whatever it was, it lingered just under the surface, barely noticeable if you didn't have a hint of that sinister intent inside you to begin with.

His gaze remained on my mouth, then scanned my entire body as Hyde moved and slipped a little further into the crowd of crushing bodies. Heat pricked at my flesh and sweat began to produce a sleek sheen across my skin, glittering slightly in the bright colors of the lights. Hyde's simile grew even more seductive while he watched, and in my mind, I continued to remind her that sex with this man was not an option. She would get the kill she wanted, but that was where she wanted ended. We shared this body, but I had rules—rules that she had agreed to that she better remember. Hyde raised my arm, and motioned toward him, beckoning him closer as she licked her lips. The man lifted his beer, took a swig, and did just as she requested with beer in hand swinging at his side with each long stride. I felt her growl deep in our throat, feeling each muscle movement deep in my bones. I wanted to take control—to leave—but that would just mean I'd owe her even more later on, and I wasn't about to give her more than was already agreed to.

We were a partnership now—uneven if you asked me—but no one was doing that, were they?

The man approached, and as soon as he was close enough, he reached out and ran his palm across my belly toward my hip—as if he were worshipping me without even knowing me. Hyde took his beer, the bottle cold and slick against our shared fingertips, and raised it to her mouth—taking a massive swallow of the bitter, hoppy liquid. Her tongue traced the lip of the bottle before handing it back to him. The lust in his eyes was instant, flaring to life behind his baby blues. Hyde's desire for the animalistic action of sex as well as the kill was hard to ignore, and inside I shook my head knowing it wouldn't do any good. She wouldn't be listening.

His large hand roamed over my body as he moved to stand behind me, pulling my hips backward so they ground into him. Warm breath slithered along the skin of my neck, tracing along my earlobe when he leaned into me and placed his lips against my ear.

"I bet that dress would look even better on my floor," he almost sang harmoniously.

Hyde looked back at him, letting the heat fill her gaze and pour into him, still moving along to the beat while raking fingers through our hair.

Hyde pushed out my lips in a fake, sexy pout. "But you'd look so good tied up to my four-poster bed." Tilting her hips back, her ass ground into his crotch, and he almost hissed with excitement. "All tied up with my red silk." She turned us to face him. "If you want to play, all my toys are at my place."

His lips parted and his breathing came in ragged, aroused pulls. I could even feel his erection against my abdomen. She thrilled in it, and I just wanted to shrink away. The look on his face left me in awe of how easily she could entice them and drawing male attention had always been easy enough for me without her in control.

Now, with her at the wheel, the pull of her was pretty much instantaneous.

Taking a deep breath, he replied, "Sounds like what I hoped for, some real fun. Your place, it is."

Then a victorious smirk lifted the corners of his mouth. Hyde reached up, took his jaw in her strong grip, and ran the very tip of our tongue over his parted lips—slipping inside just a fraction. Enough to entice, but nothing more. His sharp intake of breath told her everything she needed to know.

She had him.

Taking his hand, she led him through the crowd, and then through the New York City streets until they came to my apartment building. It stood tall, looming, and sinister as Hyde guided the man into it, and then into the elevator.

As soon as the elevator doors closed, the man gripped our waist and pushed us against the wall—gripping our wrists so he could pay attention to, well, everything. He started in on Hyde's lips, penetrating grossly with his tongue, but Hyde loved it. If I could have turned any of the sensations off to myself completely, I would have. It was unpleasant considering I knew exactly what the outcome would be. He moved down to Hyde's neck, licking, sucking, and biting.

Biting a little too hard if you asked me. The sting of his teeth made Hyde cry out and hiss as arousal pierced up from between the legs we shared and into our core. She reached down and placed her hand against the very obvious erection beneath the denim of his jeans. With a growl, he bit harder, causing a shriek and gasp of pleasure to roll through my body.

A loud ding let us know that we were on my floor, and when the doors opened, the hallway was empty. It always seemed to be, but I didn't care. It kept prying eyes down to a minimum, especially when I knew death would be knocking on our door shortly. Hyde linked a finger through one of the belt loops on his pants and tugged him along behind her.

"This is a nice place," he slurred as soon as the door opened.

"Sssssssh, don't say a word," Hyde crooned and growled all at the same time. "I only want to hear you scream."

He obviously didn't understand exactly what she meant, not like I did, because he grinned seductively and walked right into the living room and stopped at the end of the sectional. Slamming the door behind us, Hyde strode over to him, undoing the zipper on the back of the dress so she could quickly remove it from her shoulders and slide it down her body. Once it was on the floor, she quickly stepped over it as the man stared at her hungrily. Heels clicked audibly on the stone floor as she approached him, and I watched in rapt fascination as well as sickly disgust, wondering what she would do next. I had to admit that no matter how much I really hated what she did, there was a part of me that was captivated by it as well.

She pushed him back onto the couch and straddled him, moving lithely like a large cat, instincts in tune and perfect. I felt the desire for the blood—for the kill—roll through the mind we shared and waited.

The metallic tang of blood hit my tongue before I even noticed that she had bit down hard into the flesh of his neck. Not over the jugular or anything. That would have been too much of a mess to clean up off the living room couch and a lot less fun than what she had in mind in the little red room of terrors.

He screamed, sending a thrill through our chest, and pushed us with all he had until we flew backward and hit the floor. Pain ricocheted through our spine, but it didn't stop her fun. The pain lasted maybe a second, just long enough for the screaming and flailing man to get off the couch and attempt to run for the door. Hyde was up in a flash, and she lashed out, catching him in the face so he went tumbling down, spraying blood on the floor.

His feeble attempt to crawl away almost made me feel bad for him, but then I saw it again. Whatever it was in these men that she sought. Something that lingered just under the surface, only detectable to Hyde. It was there, practically radiating off of him as fear and rage met inside him. He wouldn't get a chance to use that rage to save himself. Not even close, and I had a feeling he knew it.

Hyde followed the trails of his blood left on the floor, reaching him in record time. Leaning down, she took a handful of his blond locks in her fist and pulled his head back so that he had no choice but to look at her. Tears streamed down his face, streaking through the blood splattered there like a macabre painting. His eyes were a paler blue than I originally thought now that I actually got to see them through Hyde's guise, and they were wide. Terrified beyond anything he had ever experienced before, with the evil inside just underneath. I wasn't certain what actually made the man evil—a deed or something else—but Hyde didn't care. That was all she saw when it came down to it, and I wasn't about to object to her killing him. If she didn't kill him and have her feast, she would continue to disrupt the life I was trying to have outside of her desire to maim and kill.

"Oh, come on. Didn't you want to have *some real fun?* Are you not having fun because I certainly am?" she asked, practically taunting him.

"You fucking bitch," he spat through gritted teeth.

"Now, that's just rude. That's no way to speak to a fucking lady," she chided him playfully. She pointed at him and reprimanded, "You, sir, are an asshole."

Turning on her heels, Hyde began to make her way to the bedroom where her murder room was hidden, dragging him by the hair. He tried to detangle her fingers while attempting to get clumsily to his feet, but his attempts were fruitless. Instead, he decided to start screaming again, which made Hyde more irritated than anything. I felt her roll our eyes.

"God, do you men ever shut up?"

She turned around and sent a fist into his face, effectively breaking his nose while rendering him unconscious.

She began to drag him again as if he weighed nothing and beamed.

"That's better."

# ROOTS OF DECEIT  Kindra Sowder

# CHAPTER FOUR

It took no effort at all for Hyde to drag the man by his hair into her hidden murder room, walls painted red to hide anything missed during clean up. She had practically slammed his unconscious body onto the metal slab of a table she used, tying him down rather effectively with the leather straps that reminded me of those you saw in old movies at the asylum.

As she turned away from his prone form, she removed the gorgeous bra and threw it through the threshold to land limply on the hardwood floor of the bedroom. Reaching up to the hook on the inside of the door, she pulled down the white lab coat and black rubber apron. It was that moment I began to think about how she was going to ruin yet another pair of fabulous shoes. After the thought passed through our shared mind, she did something I didn't expect. She slipped out of each high-heeled shoe and tossed them out along with the bra before shutting and locking the door.

The soft brush of fabric felt like fire against my skin, but I knew it was because of the thrill. It always sent a blazing heat through me, even when Hyde wasn't dominant, so it wasn't a surprise that it was even more vibrant tonight. Hyde moved with a quickness I had never seen, as if she were waiting an eternity to be set free so she could enact her malevolent anguish on the world.

It wouldn't exactly be a lie. I had somehow managed to lock her away for a few weeks while remaining in Emmett's near constant presence the entire time. This was her only free moment.

Her fingers nimbly tied the apron at her back before she hit the power button on a stereo I had never seen. Of course, I didn't go in the room if Hyde wasn't the dominant party. Blaring hard rock exploded from the speakers, the woman's gravelly voice penetrating Hyde's own darkness with her lyrics of death and the coming of the big bad wolf. My mind flashed to the moments in the old warehouse where I had been tortured and raped, finally able to break free with Hyde's help to rain Hell down on the men that hurt us. She called them little piggies, and she was the wolf who'd come to blow their houses down. She didn't only do that, she salted and burned the Earth with them too, killing them with so much fire and rage it was startling. I let her do it. I let her take whatever time she wanted because I also wanted revenge but wasn't strong enough at the time to do it myself.

She was my savior in a way, so that was why I struck the deal with her.

We were partners. No, strike that. We *are* partners.

Closing her eyes, she absorbed the words and the harsh notes of the song—until it was shattered by the man's screams when he awoke and realized he was strapped to a metal slab. I caught a glimpse of the crimson ceiling as she rolled her eyes again. He screamed far too much for her liking, especially since the true fun hadn't begun yet. She loved a screamer. Their shrill cries always sent a thrill through her, but only when she was actually causing them harm. Anything before was annoying beyond reproach, and I felt the urge to shut him up run through my brain, but she resisted. Killing him now just to shut him up would take the excitement out of the entire thing.

Deciding quickly to ignore him until she was upon him, she glided to the black armoire in the room and swung the doors open—putting a finger up to her lips as if in thought. Fingernail tapped against teeth while she mulled over the choice of tools at her disposal. Images of them flashed through our shared mind as or shared eyes took in the sight of gleaming metals and clean plastics—electric knife, ball-ping hammer, bone saw, needle-nose pliers, and a vast array of other hand tools and torturous devices. It was that moment that she realized she definitely needed to envision more creative devices for her room of tortures. A Judas Cradle, maybe. She imagined two-by-fours angled to meet in a point, a pyramid of iron sitting on top of it. That was something I had never seen before, so I was certain she had been looking new plans up while in complete control—the moments my vision was black and I was completely unaware.

The thought of the Judas Cradle made me shiver with disgust and fear so I severely hoped she'd give up on the thought of it, especially considering how difficult that would be to construct. At least, I thought it would be.

Her thoughts drowned out the man's screaming long enough for her to decide on what device to begin with. Reaching into the alcove of the armoire, she picked up something smooth, and it gleamed evilly in the lights of the room. It was something that I had never seen in the room before, and something no one would believe could be useful in the art of murderous torture. Something so innocent that even I would have run from the room screaming at the sight of it in that room if I could.

A melon baller.

There were only so many things she could go after with it when it came to the human body—the male body especially.

The handle was black and textured kind of like gritty sandpaper to ensure a better grip, and the metal scoop on the end glimmered—more threatening than anything else in the cabinet for unknown reasons.

*Jesus,* I thought, which only made Hyde skip along toward the table with glee.

Rolling the melon baller between her fingers, she crooned, "Oh, Blythe, you're just as sick as I am. The sooner you figure it out, the better off you'll be."

*Yeah, okay. Sure.*

The nameless man looked up at her, his face twisted in terrorized confusion at the sight of me seemingly talking to myself. If only he knew.

"What the Hell? Who the fuck—?" He started.

"I'm just talking to my inner-Psycho, dear. Nothing to be concerned about."

"Oh, God," he started before breaking out into uncontrollable sobbing, something neither her nor myself had expected.

We expected cursing and hatred, but not this, which almost made me feel sorry for him. Almost. I could still sense what Hyde did, and that changed my perspective on the entire thing exponentially.

Motioning around the room with blatant irritation, Hyde said, "If you haven't noticed, God is not in this room. So, if you could keep that God and Jesus crap to yourself, that would be great, because neither are here to save you. They see nothing, and soon, neither will you." She looked down at him, seeing his wide eyes rimmed with tears, face red and neck straining. "And if you could stop blubbering like an idiot, I can take cutting out your tongue off my list of things to do."

Hyde moved on him like a viper before he had a chance to beg for his life, placing the melon baller right in the crevice of his orbital socket, and pressing down so the small cup enveloped the top portion of the beautiful blue orb. His screaming grew louder, almost drowning out the music in the background. I felt the sensations of his moving chest, and how the metal scoop sickeningly moved inside the eye socket. Then there was the snap of the optic nerve that ran from the eye to the brain as she continued to push it behind the eye for removal—it felt like a thin rubber band snapping after being stretched out too far. Most of all, I could smell the blood in the air as it poured down the side of his face and onto the metal table.

It barely took a few minutes before she pulled the tool away from the crying, screaming man—the eyeball sitting perfectly in the scooper, staring up at us as we both stared down on it. And it was nothing like in the movies. This was the first eye she had ever removed from a victim, so I definitely was not prepared for the sight of it. It wasn't perfectly round—not like you'd expect—meat from inside his head clung to it, and the optic nerve hung from the back of it like a disgusting, bloody tendril with a sheath of gore around it.

If Hyde weren't in complete control, I probably would have vomited on the floor right then and there.

Taking the orb between her fingers, she lifted it from the scoop and inspected it, giving it a slight squeeze as if she were curious. It gave a little under the pressure, but not so much I thought she'd pop it. I cringed inside of her, and she smiled, letting lose a slight giggle.

"Don't be such a little girl, Blythe," Hyde chided a little as she tossed the eyeball into the air and caught it, moving to stand closer to the table to show the man her handiwork. She turned it in her fingers so that it was disgustingly staring down at him, and her grin grew wider when she saw his horrified expression. "God, you're just as bad as she is."

"Please, let me go. I won't tell anyone, I swear," he cried out.

Little did he know mercy was a far-away dream. There would be no such thing in that room tonight. Not even a modicum of it would make itself known, and his last breaths would take place in that room. No one would seem him alive again. Of course, no one would see him dead since Hyde was an expert at forensic countermeasures. A body was never located, which was more than could be said for the serial killer out there who was leaving bodies lying around like bloody treasures. Lauren had warned of him once, but I hadn't given him much thought until that very moment.

"Oh, here we go with the begging to be set free bit. You all say the same thing over and over. It's like a broken record with different voices stuck in one skipping spot. Well, I have to tell you something. Inflicting pain is not my vise so I'm not going to apologize for letting you know you won't get that lucky." Trailing a finger down his arm, she glanced at the eyeball in her fingers, and grinned sadistically.

"Here's lookin' at you, kid," she said in her best impersonation of Humphrey Bogart.

Crazed laughter moved through the space, overpowering the man's sobs that grew louder and louder. Setting the eye on the table beside his head, she twirled the melon baller between her lithe fingers, and slammed it down on the table—causing him to jump in the restraints.

"You know what's wrong with everyone today . . .?" she sneered down at him before turning to go back to the armoire for another weapon. I saw the flash of steel in her mind before she reached out. "Name!"

"I-it's . . . D—D—David," he stammered.

"Thank you," Hyde said, rotating on her heels as our shared hand gripped the handle of the massive butcher knife that gleamed in the lights. "You know what's wrong with everyone today, David?"

Sauntering up to the slab, she ran her fingers along the dull side of the blade, then ran a fingertip at the tip enough to where it caused a dip in the pad, but nothing else.

Sensing she wanted him to actually reply, he stuttered, "Wh—wha—what's that?"

A tear trailed down his temple as he was clearly in shock, Hyde did not seem to care but she very

quickly wiped away his tear with her forefinger—
dipping the finger into her mouth. It was strong, salty,
and permeating, like I could feel his grief and his fear
concentrated in the tiny drop of water.

"They're all just a bunch of whining, crying,
fucking pussies," she barked through gritted teeth
before raising the gigantic knife over her head and
striking down before David could shout again.

# CHAPTER FIVE

Buzzing on my bedside table roused me from sleep, and when I opened my eyes, they were almost completely crusted over. What I didn't expect was how clean me and my bed were, considering how Hyde typically left things in a bloody mess aside from the dead bodies and the room. Those were always taken away and the room left pristine. This was definitely a good change—no congealed blood between my fingers and toes, and no dried and crusty filth all over my bedsheets, clothes, and skin.

This was welcome.

What wasn't was the insistent buzzing against the wood of my bedside table.

"Oh my God, will you stop?" I shouted toward the sound.

It wasn't until I sat up that I realized it was my cell phone vibrating. Picking it up, I double-tapped the screen, and it lit up with a notification. I slid my thumb over the cool, smooth glass, and opened the text message that flashed across it—squinting past the light in my darkened bedroom. The shades had been drawn completely, which was a relief in and of itself.

A frustrated sigh left me involuntarily as soon as I saw who the text message was from.

Cyra.

*Wakey, wakey, sunshine. You have mail. Check outside your door.*

"Jesus, what now?"

Sitting my phone back down on the table, I rose to my feet and felt every joint in my body pop as I made my way to the door leading into my apartment. I was sluggish. It was as if every part of me were somewhat paralyzed, making the trek to the door even more grueling. Another relieving sight caught my eye when I approached the door. It was locked. The chain and the deadbolt were in place. Something else Hyde never bothered to do. Even the living room was perfect. Almost too perfect.

"Finally, you've learned. It only took how many years?"

I felt a shift in my mind and my belly then, as if she were answering me.

I passed a mirror on the way in the living room, and green eyes with a grin on lips that looked just like mine came into view. I froze for a moment, catching my reflection as it winked and smirked. Irritation flared in my chest, and I rolled my eyes.

"Show off," I muttered to myself, knowing she could perceive it.

If I didn't know better, I would have said I felt her snicker inside of me when I unlocked the door and flung the door open.

A massive man in a horrid brown suit stood on the other side with his hand raised like he was about to knock on the door, eyes wide with shock. His hair was clipped so short I almost thought he was bald, and the goatee kind of made him look like a douchebag, but the fact that he wasn't intimidating in the least didn't stop me from taking a stunned step backward. In his other hand, I spotted a thin vase filled halfway with water holding a single red rose with a card on a plastic holder alongside it.

I knew exactly who it was from as soon as I saw it, which made me even more frustrated that this stranger had picked up my gorgeous, private message. His grimy, sausage fingers smudged the clean glass. Well, was clean. Cringing internally, I crossed my arms over my chest and huffed.

"Can I help you?" I asked, making certain my exasperation was evident.

"Yes, ma'am," he reached into the pocked inside his gross suit jacket. "I'm looking for a," he paused to look at a notepad, "Ms. Blythe McAlister?"

"You've found her. What can I do for you . . .?"

He pulled something out of his pocket and flashed a police badge, the word 'detective' was even more frightening than it should have ever been. My heart seized in my chest and my breath caught in my lungs, panic settling in.

No, Hyde was always so careful. He couldn't be here because of us. Right?

Internally, I was screaming, but on the outside I was calm, cool, collected. Just like anyone would expect from the innocent. My body remained frozen like a deer in headlights, but it was as if he hadn't noticed at all as he flipped the thing closed and stuff it back into his suit jacket pocket.

"I'm Detective Bell with the NYPD," he said with a distinct Boston accent.

My eyebrows rose with interest, and I pointed to the vase in his hand.

"Do detectives make a habit of picking up someone's mail in Boston?" I asked, making certain he could sense my sarcasm. "Because, unless you moonlight as a delivery boy, it's kind of rude." I did my best to smile as if making a small joke at his expense.

He looked down at his hand, almost stunned, and handed it to me awkwardly.

"Oh, I'm sorry. It was sitting out here and . . . well, I haven't been here long and didn't want someone coming along and snatching it." He led the rest with a sheepish shrug. "I'm sorry."

Placating a smile to ensure I remained seemingly innocent, I took the vase from him, and said, "It's okay. I appreciate that."

"It was really no problem, Ms. McAlister."

"Blythe, please. And what can I do for you, Detective?"

I noticed his breath smelled of bad coffee and stale, cheap cigarettes when he spoke. I did my best to keep my composure as I knew I must look as though I just woke up myself.

"Right to the chase, huh?" he joked.

"You bet."

Stuffing his hands in his pockets, a gun flashed in his hip holster, and he said, "Okay. You were seen leaving club Avant Gardner with a man named James David Master last night, and his roommate said he never came home. Can you tell me what happened when you left with him?"

I worked another grin and tilted my head. "So, that was his name. We didn't exactly talk much."

Hyde's warmth erupted in my belly like a punch to the gut, but I breezed past it, answering his question.

"Yes, ma'am. That is his name."

His face went stern, determination in his stance. He wanted to find James Master, and he thought I was the key. I could see it. He wasn't exactly wrong, but I was not about to give myself—and Hyde to an extent—up. Not easily. I would suffer the consequences of her latest slay, and that wasn't in my plans.

"We fucked, Detective. I came. He came. Then he left. That's it," I stated very matter-of-factly. "Blunt enough for you? Was that what you were looking for?"

I wanted to leave no room for doubt.

"I'm so sorry, Ms. McAlister. I didn't mean to pry," he apologized. "It's just part of the job and at times, it does tend to get . . . too personal."

I crossed my arms over my chest again with the vase still gripped rightly in my hand, trying not to smoosh the delicate flower it held.

"But you did, Detective. I know that, and you know that. So, let's drop the pretenses here. You had questions, and I answered this one to the best of my knowledge. Wherever he went or whatever happened to him happened after I lost sight of him beyond this door, I don't know." I cocked my heard toward the door I leaned against. "All I know is, we had a good time, and that's that. So, if you don't mind, I'd really love to get to my first cup of coffee. Without it, I'm just a bit cranky."

"Yes, of course, I understand. I would like to give you my card and if you remember anything more, please call me." He handed me his card which had all his pertinent information printed, including his dispatch number. Detective Bell dipped his head to nod slightly, then said, "Have a good day, Ms. McAlister."

"You too, Detective. I hope you find him. He seemed like a nice guy."

"Thank you. He'll likely turn up. Likely just found a place to sleep and has not made it back home yet. Good day, Miss McAlister."

"Bye."

I waved and smiled at him as he walked toward the waiting elevator. I watched him until he disappeared into it, the mark of a seasoned cop in his swagger as he moved. The grungy suit didn't help him in the least, but everyone knew a cop's salary wasn't the best. And they especially couldn't afford a good suit to go along with their title. I couldn't help but think he would have been better off with a white button-up and black slacks, but that was just me. Either way, the appearance of Detective Bell could become a problem.

Hyde moved in my chest, and I felt her urge to speak gurgling up in my throat. I swallowed past it and moved back into the apartment, shutting the door behind it. I had fully intended on opening the card that came with the red rose, but as soon as my eyes met the mirror, it was obvious Hyde had something to say. My reflection was set in urgent determination, and I sighed.

"What?" I asked her, knowing somehow she would answer.

"He'll be back. He caught our scent, Blythe," my reflection's lips moved, and my own devilish voice came from an invisible presence beside me.

"I know, okay? I could tell. Any good detective can smell a killer a mile away. We just need to tackle one thing at a time, all right?" I picked the card from its holder and waved it at the mirror. "Adam Burnside is just as urgent, and you know that."

With a glare, she responded, "Adam Burnside isn't going to put us up for the death penalty when we're caught."

# ROOTS OF DECEIT  K|NDRA SOWDER

"I'm reading the card now," I huffed, walking away from the mirror and my own judgmental gaze. "I liked it better when you were only in my head."

*I heard that.*

In my head this time.

"Of course, you did."

Moving back into my bedroom and stepping into the walk-in closet—I had to get ready for work—I set the vase down on the table beside the mirror. The paper was smooth, elegant, and when I removed the small card, the writing was in Adam Burnside's elegant script.

*You're invited* were the first words I read, and I had to stop the groan that tried to force its way past my lips.

"A masquerade party? How cliché is that?" I asked aloud.

"It could be fun," Hyde purred.

I glanced up at my reflection and saw her staring down at the reflected invitation, a playful smirk playing at the corners of her mouth.

"It's tomorrow night," I barked.

"And? The whole masked, anonymous thing is," she paused, licking her lips, "hot. Plus, you already have so many dresses to choose from."

"Don't be crazy. There's no way he's going to introduce himself to me at a fucking party."

"Crazy is my middle name, Blythe. Remember that."

Tossing the card onto the table beside the case, I said, "I guess we're going, then. I'm getting ready for work, and you better behave in there." I tapped on my temple.

"Always," Hyde said, showing way too many teeth.

# CHAPTER SIX

The gallery was quiet except for Lauren's clicking heels as she paced in front of me, fidgeting with her manicured fingernails. She had almost worn off the white, French tips already.

Glancing up from my own small sketch pad, I chided, "You're going to have to get those nails redone. They look like Cujo got ahold of them."

Stopping abruptly, she looked at her nails, and then to me, the nervousness plain in her features.

"You're not nervous?" she asked.

I shrugged. "Why should I be? Granted, Emmett didn't tell me about this, but that's what the brooding artist types tend to do."

She leered at an invisible bystander. I went back to my work. She continued to pace around like she was lost in our area of the gallery.

"He never told you him and Cyra were working on a collection together?"

"No, but it's not like I asked about any projects either. New relationship, and all." I waved a dismissive hand in the air. "I was trying not to pry."

Lauren scoffed, "Maybe you should have."

# ROOTS OF DECEIT  Kindra Sowder

"Maybe," I replied nonchalantly.

We had just gotten the news that morning, Hannah letting us know that the paintings would be arriving for mine and her approval for an exhibition, that she knew would turn into sales. I was shocked, but not all at once. It was as I told Lauren. The artist types were all about their secrets. Even I could attest to that. Some were well worth keeping under lock and key.

"Well," Lauren huffed again, crossing her arms over her chest, "hopefully it's worth it."

"Hannah says it is."

I heard Lauren mutter my words under her breath. I only sighed, placing my piece of charcoal on the pad, setting it down on the receptionist's desk—who was thankfully absent—and removed a wipe from my bag at my side to clean the black from my fingers. Just as I glanced up, I saw Emmett push through the doors with Cyra and Jackson in tow. A big truck stopped on the street out front—double-parked, of course.

When his large brown eyes met mine, he beamed, but that quickly dissipated when he spotted the irritation in my face.

Standing up, I approached him and took his arm, guiding him off to the side.

"Hey, Bly—" Cyra began.

"Not now," I cut her off and ignored her.

Her I could deal with later.

Gritting my teeth, I spoke as quietly as I could to avoid prying ears.

"What the Hell happened to you? You completely bailed on me during dinner, and then you never came by," I hissed as soon as I turned to face him.

His face fell. There was no anger there—only regret—which made me want to take my anger back, but I still couldn't.

"I'm really sorry. I wanted to tell you, but this project was top secret. And…" he paused, licking his sensuous lips, "something went wrong with one of the paintings in the collection. I'm sorry."

"So, it was Cyra that texted you?" I asked skeptically.

"Yes." He bobbed his head and reached up to move my hair lovingly away from my face. "Did you think I was with another woman?"

"No, of course not," I replied as my heart pounded rapidly in my chest. It was an absolute lie, and I had a feeling he could sense it. "We never said we were exclusive."

"Do you want to be? I mean . . . exclusive, I mean?"

# ROOTS OF DECEIT   Kindra Sowder

I was a strong woman—independent—but for some reason I couldn't look at him. I couldn't look into that beautiful face that only made my knees weak and my walls crumble. Hyde even enjoyed his company enough not to force her presence and kill him, which was always a good sign. My entire body hummed and sang with his presence even though I felt eyes on my back as we spoke animatedly. Despite all of my strengths, I found myself speechless. He was asking me if I wanted exclusivity. How could I answer it without seeming greedy? He was an amazing man—moody lately—but that was easily explainable knowing what I knew now.

"Blythe?" His eyes betrayed him, showing concern.

He hooked a finger under my chin and forced my eyes to his face, his own orbs glittering with admiration and something more underneath I couldn't place. His finger was so smooth against my skin, and hot like the first of our passion for one another literally blazed within him.

I smoldered beneath his touch and my entire body lit up from the one point of contact. Hyde made her presence known, flaring through my core as each nerve fiber ignited.

"If exclusivity is what you want, I can give that to you. All you have to do is say yes, and I'm all yours, baby."

So many promises spilled out of those words, and I didn't hesitate this time when I answered.

"Yes, I do," I whispered.

"So do I, so there it is. We're exclusive. Sound good to you?" He grinned down at me, eyes warm, and my knees almost melted out from underneath me.

"Okay," I sighed with relief, staring up at him with bright eyes that made me feel like a love-struck idiot. "Sounds good."

"So, maybe now we can head in the back and take a look at what I have to offer, huh?"

A lump formed in my throat, and when someone—Lauren—cleared her throat behind us, I snapped back into reality. We were at the gallery. I cursed under my breath and turned to look at her, attempting to hide the glare I felt furrowing my eyebrows.

Shooting a mournful glance at Emmett, my face turned stern and cold, and I said, "Yes, let's try to be professional. Shall we, Mr. Adler?"

I gestured with my hand toward the back show room where a parade of heavily-muscled men brought in painting after painting covered in a protective layer of thick plastic and brown paper. Each man wore an ugly khaki uniform like those that worked with moving companies wore. Jose was there as well, directing them with his subtle demeanor.

Emmett chuckled and went in the same direction as the men, disappearing through an open threshold. Lauren's eyebrows lifted with genuine interest as she watched me. A flush crept up my cheeks, which wasn't typical for me. I didn't get embarrassed, but this man— this stubborn, gorgeous man—turned me into a teenaged girl. One that just happened to have a killer lingering inside of her.

"What?" I nearly shrieked at her.

Coming toward me, she stopped just within earshot, and asked, "What the Hell was that? A lover's spat?"

"Good God, no, Lauren. It was not. Now, if you don't mind, get Hannah so we can take a look at this stuff, okay? I know she wanted her eyes on the collection too," I ordered, ignoring the shit-eating grin on her face.

Lauren's eyes bore into me, and I felt playful irritation grow in the pit of my stomach as she began to walk away and toward Hannah's office. The glee was too evident in her face, and she was practically skipping on her platform heels.

"Blythe's got a boyfriend," she chimed in a sing-song voice while tilting her head from side to side like a child in the school yard making fun of her friend with a crush on a boy.

"Shut up, will you? Go on," I shooed her with my hands. "Get!"

She mocked a frown. "You're mean."

"Don't make me get the whip next, little girl," I joked.

Lauren, being as playful as always, put her index finger to her lips and winked at me before she started walking again but not before smacking her right ass cheek and smiling broadly.

"That's my favorite, and you know it."

As we both laughed, we headed in opposite directions—her toward Hannah's office, and me toward the show room where I was certain I may not like what I was about to see.

The unload and hanging of the paintings, plus reveals took most of the day. I felt some exhaustion in my calves from the heels I wore but with Emmett around, I never felt better. It was as though I drew more resilience with his presence. Hyde stirred at my need to just sit down and wanted to speak up but I stifled that quickly. I did not need her input to get through my day. She needed to just continue to behave as promised.

# CHAPTER SEVEN

"Well, you two, I can say I pictured a lot of things when your benefactor contacted me," Hannah said, pausing as she stood in front of one of the paintings, studying it. "But I didn't expect this."

"It's definitely something," Lauren sighed. "What do you think, Blythe?"

I stood in stunned silence, Emmett at my side while Cyra stood closer to the pieces as they leaned against the white wall. If anyone asked me to describe what I saw, there were no words I could use to do so elegantly. The images were a mixture of splashes of color shattered by splattered red paint, practically decapitating any figure on the canvas they lay underneath. I could feel the violence in them—the pain—especially the longing buried underneath. They were scarred, just like their creators. Without glancing at anyone, I walked up to one that spoke to me the loudest, leaning forward until my nose was mere inches from the canvas before closing my eyes. The only smell to permeate my senses was the scent of fresh paint.

My eyes snapped open, only seeing the marring slash of red against the other stark colors. A sense of familiarity hit me then, punching me square in the chest as my vision blurred into just a streak of crimson. I held in the shocked gasp as images of Hyde's kills slashed their way into my waking memory. Swallowing hard, I stood up, took a step back from them, and attempted to remain as calm as I could while pretending to look at the canvases objectively.

"It's violent, more violent than either of your other stuff, but I think we can work with this," I explained. "To the right market, we can clean house."

Emmett and Cyra's eyebrows both shot up in confused interest while Lauren's sinister smile surfaced, and Hannah began to nod while looking at another canvas closest to her. The painting had a very subtle outline of a woman with splashes of a deeper blue, red streak across the middle of the elusive form.

"And what market is that?" Cyra asked, crossing her arms over her chest skeptically.

"The hardcore market," Hannah stated very matter-of-factly, face certain.

"You mean BDSM?" Cyra almost shrieked.

A beat of silence moved through the room for a moment before I took a step away from the painting I had been studying, turned to the group, and grinned with pride.

"Among other things." My tone was serious, and it was aimed at Cyra who one would think would be more attuned to such things but apparently was not.

Emmett began to chuckle with a nod as if he agreed with my assessment. Cyra looked shocked, but I knew better than to believe that anything truly shocked her working for Adam Burnside. Considering what she had told me about him and some of the literature shared with me, she knew a lot more about things of this nature than she was willing to admit. Plus, I was certain Emmett didn't have as much to do with the overall content of the collection itself since his previous work had been mostly erotic instead of horrifying—unlike Cyra's. It led me to believe he laid down the groundwork, and Cyra elaborated. It wasn't exactly a surprising revelation, if I were going to be honest about the entire thing. But it did make me wonder who approached who about the project to begin with.

"So, Blythe, you'll run with this one, then? I have a feeling you know just what to do to drum up the publicity needed for a collection like this," Hannah said. "And Lauren can take second on this. Fill this place with strapping men and women draped in leather and latex if that's what it takes to sell them all. I know it won't be a problem for you."

73

"Oh my God, can I?" Lauren asked, almost jumping up and down and clapping with excitement. "Blythe, this one will be so much fun."

"It will be," I responded, my eyes meeting Emmett's that seemed to smolder—him becoming fidgety like he had the night before.

"So, is that a yes?" Hannah questioned.

With a nod, gaze never leaving Emmett's, I replied, "It's a yes, Hannah."

"Goody," she said, clapping her hands once before beginning to walk back toward her office. "I trust you all can get started as soon as possible without supervision. Lauren, please come with me. I want you to run down my list of established contacts and see what kind of audience we can possibly draw among our regulars."

"Y-yeah," Lauren stuttered, "I'm coming."

She followed quickly, heels clicking erratically on the hardwood floor as she struggled to keep up with Hannah who was already halfway to her office. Laughing a little, I turned back to the paintings and felt Emmett and Cyra both watching me, Emmett's eyes burning into my profile as I stared at one painting in particular.

# ROOTS OF DECEIT  Kindra Sowder

The background figure was a woman, another in the foreground a muscular man—both overlaid with greens and blues and sliced with that slash of red, which was already becoming far too familiar.

After a few seconds, it began to draw me in, and I almost completely zoned out before Emmett's fingers traced down the back of my arm. The sensation sent a chill down my spine, proceeded by a blazing heat between my legs and in my stomach. Hyde stirred, and I held my breath to drown her out. She barely receded, as I let the breath out slowly. His lips grazed my ear, and the sensual growl he made would have been nearly imperceptible if he weren't right next to me.

"I'll see you later, baby. Maybe I'll have something leather waiting for you at your apartment," he whispered, promising untold pleasures we had yet to experiment with.

"You promise?" I whispered I return, turning my head so I could nuzzle against the stubble on his jaw.

His breath caught in his throat. "You bet."

Heat flooded my entire body from head to toe, and when I could tell he noticed, he smiled proudly to himself and took a step back.

"I'll see you later."

# ROOTS OF DECEIT  Kindra Sowder

Watching him walk away, I waved my goodbye only to hear Cyra's knowing laughter. I turned to see her standing near one of the larger paintings, arms crossed over her chest as she watched mine and Emmett's interactions. The smirk on her face said it all without her having to say a single word, and all it did was make me smile right back at her with the same expression. Mocking sincerity. That was the only way I knew to describe that look. Maybe a little contempt as well, but Cyra had always been more snide than anything—never contemptuous.

"That's so cute. You guys are really made for each other," she teased.

"You don't have somewhere else to be?" I asked with the same, frothy tone.

Tilting her head, she seemed to think about it for a moment, and then shook her head. "Nope, but I do have a message from Adam for you."

"And you had to do that here?" I gestured toward the show room with both hands, anger rising in my throat.

"Why not?" she said, still smirking, as she slowly made her way toward me—eyes penetrating despite her bright pink hair. "Oh, I get it. You want to keep your secret . . ." she leaned forward and whispered, "a secret."

"If you have a message from Adam, Cyra, don't you think you should just give it? Don't want to piss off your benefactor, do you? He may take all your toys away."

She clicked her tongue, the frustration clear on her face, then motioned toward someone behind me. I turned to find Jackson, the massive black-clad bodyguard, standing in the doorway of the show room with his hands clasped in front of him. The sleeves of the t-shirt strained around his large biceps, dark eyes piercing as always.

"What is this?" I asked, using my thumb to point to Jackson standing behind me like he was awaiting further instruction.

"Well, Adam heard about the police presence at your apartment this morning, and he wants to make sure you're not being followed around. He wants to make sure you are protected, and Jackson will also be escorting you to the party." She walked past me, and pat Jackson lovingly on the shoulder. He only looked rather annoyed at the contact. "Make sure to wear your mask, Blythe dear. And I don't mean the one you wear in public." She eyed me over her shoulder as she walked away.

With that, she was gone, and I stood there staring at Jackson for a few heartbeats.

"So," I began awkwardly, "you're going everywhere I go?"

He nodded. "Yes, ma'am."

I scoffed at the word *ma'am* with disgust.

"Please, none of this *ma'am* business. Just call me Blythe." When he didn't say anything, the awkward feeling between the two of us began to grow. "Sorry I threatened you before."

"It's quite all right," he replied, completely monotone.

I nodded, accepting his acceptance of my apology, and began to make my way out of the room. My time at the gallery was done for the day, and I was ready to go home. I had a visit, as well as a party, to get ready for. As soon as I passed Jackson's shoulder, there was an entertained glint in his eyes.

"Where to, Miss?"

"Home. Don't we have a party to prepare for?"

He laughed, but just barely, and then followed me. "Yes, ma'am."

# CHAPTER EIGHT

A knock sounded at my front door as I stood in my bedroom in my strapless bra and panties, staring at the dress I had very hastily purchased. It was beautiful—a deep crimson with some black underlay, and strapless with an A-line bust. Reaching down to the floor, it would drag if I didn't wear stilettos, which only made the decision to wear a gorgeous pair of new Giuseppe Zanotti Cruel's with it. The dress clashed with my pale skin beautifully, and the mask I chose to go with it was simple enough. Straight black with lace on the fringes. Stunning in the way it framed my eyes. The shoes were a treat paid for with the bonus commissions I earned on Emmett's sale. While I loved wearing my Louboutin's, these were only for this function.

Jackson had vowed to stay in the living room while I got ready. Apparently, I needed protection since Detective Bell showed up at my door. I felt it was unnecessary, but Adam Burnside—the man just like me I was finally going to meet—felt vastly differently.

"Mr. Adler, it's nice to see you again," Jackson said from the living room.

# ROOTS OF DECEIT KINDRA SOWDER

My heartbeat picked up at the mention of him and a smile crept over my lips without my willing it. It was an automatic reaction. Emmett did that to me—the only issue was that Hyde was also drawn to him. Especially during those moments at the restaurant when his mood did a complete one-eighty.

Hushed words whispered their way down the hallway, followed by Emmett's very distinct and proud footfalls. As soon as I looked up, the bedroom door opened, and he filled the threshold with his large muscular body. He still wore the same clothes he had on earlier—thin white t-shirt, dark jeans, black leather jacket, and black boots to match. His short-cropped hair was tousled like he had just rolled out of bed, the stubble on his jaw so devastatingly sexy.

"Hey, you," I greeted.

The grin on his face was infectious. "Hey, beautiful."

The slight Southern drawl I heard just the night before was back, almost making me weak at the knees. He seemed more comfortable in his skin tonight as he moved into the room and closed the door behind him. Much less irritable and angry—stiff. He walked toward me, and the muscles rolled under his skin. He came to stand in front of me, running his hand over my flesh and pulling me closer to him so I was pressed against his broad chest.

"Where are you going?" he asked, obviously noticing the dress, the heels, and the mask laid out on the bed.

His stubble grazed my jaw as he nuzzled into me, the sensation sending a ripple through my entire body that settled into a radiating heat in my belly.

"Seems your benefactor is hosting a little masquerade, and I was invited," I replied. "Weren't you? Being his golden child and all?"

Pulling away from me, his hand slipped from mine while he made his way to the bed—sitting down gingerly as not to wrinkle my dress. His fingers played carefully with the soft fabric, and he grinned sheepishly. When he looked up at me again, his eyes were filled with desire and something else that lingered just underneath. Something I had seen recently, and only once. Something I couldn't quite put my finger on but felt familiar all the same. It pulled at my insides, causing Hyde to stir just enough to notice.

"I was," he paused, licking his lips, "in a fashion."

"In a fashion?" I mirrored, questioning.

He only nodded, the expression never once leaving his face.

# ROOTS OF DECEIT Kindra Sowder

"You're going to be cryptic about it?" I pushed—hands going to my hips as one hitched to the side.

"I am."

"You know I'm not the most patient person in the world, Emmett. What the Hell does *in a fashion* even mean?"

He got up from the bed and slinked toward me, stopping just within arm's reach—taking one hand and hooking it into the waistband of my panties to pull me closer.

"You'll see, I promise," he whispered not my throat, planting a light kiss that was quickly proceeded with a flick of his tongue.

My head fell back of its own accord, allowing him even more access. He took full advantage, trailing kisses and licks up my neck until he found my jaw. The groan left my lips before I could stop it. Emmett's arms came around me as he chuckled against my skin, drawing even more heat to the point where our flesh connected.

"You're an evil, evil man," I said through gasps.

He laughed again. "Yes, I am."

"You know, we can't be all sex all the time."

He pulled back and looked deep into my eyes, grinning down softly at me. His body grew tense, each muscle flexing with what little anxiety I could sense coming off him like smoke.

"How does tomorrow night sound? We can have a nice night in with take-out, and we can learn all about each other. Sound good?" he asked.

His expression was completely genuine, the hard edge in his gaze suddenly lifting away almost like it had never existed in the first place. The human part of me felt joyous thinking of the prospect of it, but I felt Hyde cringe on the inside.

*Not like you can tell him everything, Blythe,* Hyde rang in my head.

Shaking her words away, I beamed up at him, and felt like a part of my world was opening up, even if it was just a small part.

"You promise?"

"I promise," he replied, the sultry gleam in his eyes returning. "So, do we have time?"

Looking up at him, I grinned sensually, and reached in between us—rubbing the palm of my hand against him through his jeans.

"Maybe," I crooned.

A deep, resonating growl sounded in his throat before he reached around, grabbed my ass, and lifted me from the floor. I wrapped my legs around his waist and my arms around his neck, heat flicking up from between my legs and radiated out with such savagery I gasped when his jeans rubbed against my panties. He turned, and after a few steps, I felt him sit me down on the top of my dresser. His lips collided with mine and his hands roamed over every inch of my body, fingers playing with my nipples through the padding of my bra.

After that moment, I had completely forgotten that Jackson was outside the room waiting for me to emerge to go to Adam's party. In that moment, it didn't matter to me at all. I wanted Emmett more than anything I had ever wanted—well, besides freedom from my murderous alter-ego.

What he did with his hands ricocheted through my entire body, bringing heat and a delicious pain along with it. I threw my head backward, and Emmett's lips soon met my flesh, trailing kisses down until he reached my collar bone. And bit down hard. A gasp left my lips before I could stop it, but I didn't stop him. It woke something else up within me, Hyde stirring bringing another beautiful wave of energy through my womanhood and up my spine.

Emmett's lips brushed my earlobe, his breath hot in my ear.

# ROOTS OF DECEIT   KINDRA SOWDER

"I need to be inside you," he whispered.

The word *need* stirred me further, and when I looked deep in his gorgeous brown eyes, I reached down and unbuttoned his jeans with one hand. The zipper came down easily enough. so much so I barely had to touch it at all.

"Down," I ordered, and he obliged willingly.

He pushed his jeans and boxers down past his waist, not even caring about the rest of our clothes. passion entwined us and becoming in more ways than this was all that mattered. I reached out and wrapped my hand around him. His shocked and erotic gasp drove me forward, his head dropping to my shoulder. I guided him to my opening, and that was all the invitation he needed. Thrusting hard, he pushed into me so deep that my other hand gripped his shoulder, scratching the leather of his jacket instead of his skin.

Every thrust sent a ripple of pleasure through us both, his trembling body pouring more energy into our lovemaking. Neither one of us held back. I was loud, and he growled deep in his chest and throat. When his muscles tensed, his hands gripped my hips—fingers digging into my supple flesh.

# ROOTS OF DECEIT  KINDRA SOWDER

His entire body stiffened, and his head leaned back—the feeling of him convulsing inside me giving me more pleasure than anything I had ever felt before.

We were both spent, and his forehead came down to lean against mine, breath coming hard and fast as he continued to tremble with me still pulsing slightly from the intensity of my own orgasm while I was still wrapped around him. Reaching up, I ran my fingers through his hair, and kissed his cheek. We came down slowly, riding the high and the feel of each other. His lips brushed my ear again, and he said the words I did not expect, especially since we hadn't learned enough about one another yet.

"I love you," he whispered.

It didn't take any effort to say those same words back to him. The scariest part of all was that I meant them.

# CHAPTER NINE

Jackson drove along the dirty city streets of New York City, the filth and grime fading away into the richer part of the city. Manhattan was fabulous, and it was something I wasn't expecting. I was expecting anyone else like myself would love the privacy of the surrounding forests and mountains of the Upstate, but as always, Adam seemed to be full of surprises. Of course, I wasn't expecting a boisterous party either.

Everything was a haze as we drove, my vision blurring as I lost focus on the actual ride itself—thoughts floating off into the nothingness. Then it hit me. I knew nothing about this man except the basics. His name was Adam Burnside, he was the benefactor for Cyra and Emmett, he had been watching me, and he suffered a similar affliction.

At the moment that last thought crossed my mind, my reflection in the darkened window smirked with that familiar twinkle in its eye. Hyde was relishing in the entire thing but let me hold onto control for the time-being.

Turning to look at Jackson, my would-be bodyguard, driver, and supposed new bestie, all I could see was the back of his head—deep brown eyes intent on the road from the rear-view mirror.

"Hey, Jackson?" I asked.

"Yes, Ms. McAlister?" he replied.

This was my moment to learn anything I could before arriving and meeting the man face-to-face. Of course, that was if Jackson were willing to share anything with me that I could possibly use. I hated walking in unprepared, and I had been more than that for all of this.

"Mr. Burnside," I paused before continuing, "what kind of man is he?"

I saw his brow furrow in the rear-view mirror, eyes laced with confusion.

"I'm not certain what you are asking."

"Is he a good man?"

He seemed to contemplate that for a moment, each passing second causing me to regret even asking to begin with. As soon as I opened my mouth to take it back, pull the question back deep into myself, he spoke.

"He is . . ."

I could hear the hesitation.

"But . . .?"

"But, if crossed, he won't hesitate to retaliate. And he always gets what he wants, no matter what it takes."

Jackson took the next right to a street that if followed long enough would lead us out past Yankee Stadium.

"I see," was all I could say in response before turning back to look out the window.

"Is that all, Ms. McAlister?" Jackson asked.

I nodded but didn't say anything at all. Just continued to watch the buildings pass and the changes in my expression as I absorbed his words. It wasn't a lot of information, but it didn't take much to figure him out once I heard Jackson's answer.

Another thought crossed my mind.

"Jackson?"

"Yes, Ms. McAlister?" he replied, curiosity deep in his voice.

"How long have you known him? Well, worked for him?" I asked.

"It's been ten years since I started working for him."

I pondered that for a second before licking my lips and opening my mouth to ask, "How did you meet him?"

Jackson didn't respond, just continued driving— almost as if the question hadn't been uttered.

"I'm sorry. I know it's none of my business," I apologized.

"No, it's okay. I was just trying to figure out a way to make it sound better, but there really isn't one." He chuckled, adjusted in the driver's seat, and gripped the steering wheel even harder as we drove through the streets of Upper Manhattan.

His eyes moved back and forth from me to the road in the rearview mirror as if he were trying to decide if he really wanted to divulge his past to me. Adam's past. Well, a part of it. The hesitation was there, but the willingness to share was as well.

His shoulders rose, and then sagged as he took a deep breath.

"I had been a junkie. Just got out of prison doing hard time for possession and trafficking cocaine. I needed a job when Adam found me living in a half-way house. Offered me the chance to better myself. Offered amazing pay and benefits I couldn't pass up. And he'd help me stay clean as long as I worked for him. For him, it was a bonus that I could stay quiet and discreet. I had been using and dealing for years before someone sold me out," he explained. "Thanks to Adam, I've been clean ever since. I go to Narcotics Anonymous meetings and when I have a craving, he helps put it all back in perspective, so I don't give in. I have to take care of very unusual requests, but I love my job."

"What kinds of errands does he ask you to run?" I pushed a little bit further.

Jackson laughed, his shoulders shaking at the hilarity of my question. The sound floated to my ears pleasantly.

"Considering your," he paused, "similar affliction to Mr. Burnside, I'm certain you know exactly what kind of errands I run for him."

"Oh," was all I said when the words sunk in.

I knew exactly what he was asked to do. At that moment, all of the bodies found of random women made perfect sense, and it opened my eyes just a little wider to the type of man I was about to meet. Of course, I wasn't any better. My alter-ego just hid the skeletons a lot better than his.

"Is there anything else you would like to know about?" Jackson asked, eyeing me I the rearview mirror again.

My gaze dropped to the back of the leather seat in front of me. "No, that's okay."

I studied the texture of the leather—the real leather—and didn't even pay much attention to anything else. The stitching was perfect, every space between the threads even and straight. The weaving, nearly invisible veins in the leather hinted at is newness. They would grow with time, much like how the wrinkles would deepen when I grew old. If I could. It made me wonder how old Adam truly was. Cyra had stated that he was the first of his kind—our kind. Considering how far back this all seemed to go as evidenced by the journal gifted by Adam himself, his creation happened quite some time ago. I couldn't be certain just how long, but I was willing to bet it was much longer than any human being should have been expected to survive the ravages of time.

"Jackson?" I asked again, eyes snapping up so I could see him in the mirror as well as the hunch of his shoulders as he drove.

He straightened, rolling his shoulders back with the pride of his position, and cleared his throat.

"Yes, Ms. McAlister?"

I thought about it again before asking, hesitating for fear of the answer.

"How old is Adam?"

There was a long beat of silence, anxiety rising in my gut and chest as my heart raced waiting for the reply I knew could change everything. Would change everything. He was the first. To me, that could very well mean he came from ancient origins. Was that even possible? I wasn't even certain what exactly caused this genetic quirk that caused two persons to rise within one body and mind. Maybe Adam has the answer to that question too. Maybe, just maybe, I could know myself and Hyde a little better than just the little we gleaned from one another by coexisting.

"That's not for me to say. I'm sure he will tell you in his own time," was all the reply I got.

I sat there, stunned enough not to realize the car was slowing—then stopped completely. Jackson got out of the car, came around, and opened my door, putting his hand out to me.

"And here we are," he said.

I took his hand and slid out of the car, eyes staring down at the sidewalk until I finally took a moment to look up. The building was massive, and beautiful. Older, which made perfect sense considering who lived inside. I stood in awe for a moment, Jackson's hand falling away as he turned to shut the car door behind me.

"Wow," I sighed. "What floor does he live on?"

"All the way at the top," Jackson responded, standing in front of me and pointing up toward the sky.

Hyde moved inside my belly, warm and growling almost like we could both feel Adam's eyes on us from all the way up there. In a way, I could feel him. His presence was at the fringes of my awareness, pushing down on me. Not oppressive in any way. More like hovering—observing.

Jackson guided me to the front doors of the building, and I felt like my entire life was about to change. For better or worse, I had no idea, but change was coming either way. And I wasn't sure if I was ready.

# CHAPTER TEN

Adjusting the mask on around my eyes, I stood quietly with Jackson as the elevator rose to Adam's penthouse. My heart beat rapidly in my chest, and my stomach tossed and turned—anxiety creeped up into my throat, waiting escape. I swallowed hard and turned to look at Jackson beside me.

He was the picture of serenity, legs shoulder-width apart and hands clasped in front of him. The perfect bodyguard. Dressed in all black, he looked more imposing than he truly was, which I guessed was the idea behind the ensemble. Either way, I was glad he was there with me to help occupy the silence. The sound of his breathing filled the space, but nothing could drown out the sound of blood rushing in my ears.

After a few more seconds, the sound of loud rock music pushed in the crack of the elevator doors—then they opened up and unveiled a massive throng of people past the extravagant foyer.

Jackson came forward and stopped just inside the elevator doors, turning back to me, and motioning out toward the crowd with a hand.

"After you, Ms. McAlister."

# ROOTS OF DECEIT  Kindra Sowder

I stepped tentatively out, hearing the door attempt to close with Jackson in the way. Most would not have noticed but I heard my heels click on the stone floor—granite or marble, I wasn't sure. I could thank Hyde for the enhanced hearing too.

The walls were stark white, and the floors change to deep red carpet once the foyer turning into a large living room. It was a fresh, modern look—all sleek lines. It was cold, and not what I had expected. Flashing lights bounced off the white walls, reflecting in all hues like reds and blues, becoming a beautiful royal purple. Bodies writhed and moved in tandem to the thrumming guitars, slamming bass, and high feminine voice. Watching them, I felt Hyde stir inside my mind and my stomach.

*This is more like it*, I heard her growl in my head.

Ignoring her, I watched as Jackson began to move toward the crowd of people.

"I will take you to Mr. Burnside. He wanted to see you right away," he explained.

"Okay," I replied, swallowing down my anxiety again.

Scratchy male vocals weaved into the female's high cadence, turning into a melody of deep-seeded pain and regret. Of loss. Following Jackson, I moved through the foyer and into the living room, pushing past grinding bodies. The heady scent of sex and sweat filled my nostrils, making Hyde stir even more.

My eyes met those of a lovely dark woman, her chocolate skin gleaming with perspiration and glitter of unknown origin—a man against her as they rode the high of the music and whatever drug they decided to take that night. My eyes lingered there for a long moment, longer than intended, until she closed hers and allowed her head to fall back as the man held her against him.

I turned away, almost losing Jackson's large back in the crowd as they parted around him. He weaved a route for me. I still had to push past a few that drifted into my path, not paying attention to anything but the beat and their intermingled breaths as they swayed. The familiar heat began to build within my chest, and resting my palm against my breastbone, I felt Hyde beating there along with my racing heart.

She seemed just as eager as I was to meet a man who proclaimed to be the first of those with our affliction. Maybe she sensed a form of freedom on the horizon. Who knew? At the moment, I felt a mixture of wonder, curiosity, and dread. I wasn't certain which was stronger, but they all took precedence regardless.

# ROOTS OF DECEIT  Kindra Sowder

It wasn't long before we reached a hallway littered with a few couples scattered down its expanse—one or two almost to the point of intercourse, and one just getting started in what I interpreted as foreplay. A blush crept over my cheeks, but I pushed it down and averted my eyes, following the bodyguard to the very end of the hallway where a solid black door held in the secrets of the unknown.

Reaching forward, Jackson opened the door as I approached, swinging it wide. I saw mostly darkness, the light in the room so faint I could only see the outlines of furniture. Maybe a desk, a chair, but not much else.

"He'll be with you in a moment," Jackson said, ushering me inside.

I did as requested and took the few steps necessary to go inside. The moment my feet touched the carpet, Jackson shut the door, the hushed click the only sign he had done so.

The room was quiet, and my eyes worked hard to adjust to the light. With Hyde's help, it happened quickly, and I felt the blaze in my eyes as things looked a lot less like a horror film. My eyes scattered around the room, seeing the massive bookshelves that held tome upon tome—every classic you could think of, plus modern works of fiction. Some non-fictions, but not a lot. Some books on art, which had me intrigued. But then my gaze settled on the sight directly in front of me. I could make out the desk, littered with old trinkets like a vintage gyroscope, vintage globe, and a few miscellaneous office supplies. The space was rather sparse, modern. The chair behind the desk was turned away from me, and I could see the top of a dark head of hair, but nothing else.

My heart stopped for a moment, and then my heart quickened. I was about to meet the very first of my kind. I was terrified and ecstatic all at the same time, and I wasn't certain which emotion was more prominent. But that didn't really matter, did it? This moment was what mattered. Not the emotions that ran rampant through my body. Just the man sitting in the chair, turned away from me so that I couldn't see his face. Every muscle in my body began to ache from sweet tension, and Hyde became even more aware— moving through me like a tidal wave threatening to take over. She could sense something that I couldn't.

In the quickest of moments, it was as if she shared her vision with me, and I felt it for the first time. Something off.

Something evil and dark that lingered just beneath the surface. Something unimaginable that I couldn't quite put my finger on. All I felt was Hyde's reaction to it. While I myself felt terror, she felt longing. It was confusing considering what I felt coming from the other person that she helped me to feel, but I understood somehow too.

"Hello," I almost whispered, the fear of what I could possibly see choking me to near silence.

A deep, masculine bass came from the chair, but the voice was unrecognizable. It was deep and scratchy, almost as if another voice resided within it. It sent a ripple through me—through Hyde—and I felt my body almost give into the sensations that came with it.

"I was beginning to think you weren't coming," the man I took to be Adam Burnside said, voice moving deliciously through my bones. "I'm so glad you decided to attend."

Remaining as nonchalant as I could so that my intrigue didn't show, I said, "I never miss a good party, Mr. Burnside."

"I'm glad to hear that," he responded. "And I am certain that Cyra has somewhat educated you on what it is we are? What I am?"

I nodded, realizing he couldn't see it.

"Yes, she has. She said that we were a genetic anomaly. And that you were the first, but I'm still not sure what *we* are exactly."

He chuckled low in his throat, and I could feel the growl within it bring Hyde even further to the surface. A pressure began to build in my head, almost like a sinus headache that actually pounded all over—and much deeper than any pain I had ever had.

"I see it as a gift, while others see it as a curse. We are genetically blessed with being able to kill indiscriminately, but with purpose. The purpose for you may be unclear, but I have always known what I am, and what I do. From the beginning, I have been judge, jury, and executioner. Each person is different, but I feel you and I are more alike than you could imagine."

Every part of my body began to sing with horrifying, sweet, stinging energy—Hyde rising even more into my conscious mind and seeping into my very being. Every vein and nerve-ending filled to the brim with the energy she brought to the surface. The warmth, and the need coalescing into an extravagant ache.

"And why is that?" I asked, gasping and short of breath with anticipation.

"Because," Adam said as the chair began to turn so I could see his face, "you're just as thirsty for blood as I am, and that deepest part of you knows it."

The face I saw when he came to fully face me caused the blood to freeze in my veins, the building ache I felt deep inside of me exploded. I felt pain, grief, anger, sadness, horror, love, and pure rage all at once. Every memory, every single experience Hyde had pushed into the recesses of my mind came flooding back with stunning clarity. I saw my mother and father die at my hands. I saw each man I brutally murdered under the guise of another. I saw and felt the torture and agony inflicted by Adam's men that kidnapped me to avenge their friend. I reveled in the revenge I took on them.

I felt the darkness wrap itself around me like a warm blanket, and felt Hyde move within me—snapping at the bit with everything she had held onto for me. Everything she protected me from when she felt it was too much.

How could this happen? How had I—?

Emmett's face stared back at me, his beautiful browns now a stunning, almost glowing blue from beneath his luscious lashes.

## ROOTS OF DECEIT  Kindra Sowder

"I'm here to bring out that murderous vixen inside of you," he rumbled.

I couldn't stop the gasp as it left my mouth. Then, just as quickly as I had begun to understand, I knew nothing. Everything had changed.

# MISCREANT:

## A MISS HYDE ORIGIN STORY

Watching the young woman, her deep auburn hair swaying in the slight breeze as she walked in her red-bottomed high-heeled pumps, I took another puff of the cigarette. I had already allowed it to burn between my fingers for far too long. She was strikingly beautiful, toned, and gave off an air of professionalism all while something seemingly remained hidden underneath. Something only me – and others like me – could detect, although I had learned to keep my own essence from those same people.

I puffed out the bitter smoke as I continued to watch the woman who held my interest, and even though I knew little more than her name, or her occupation, I knew what she was. She knew what she was. I could see it in the way she carried herself, but there seemed to be a somber note underneath that sinister pride.

She was a monster – just as sick and horrifying as myself.

# ROOTS OF DECEIT   Kindra Sowder

While I was unrepentant, she carried guilt on her shoulders because of what I knew she had done. What she would undoubtedly continue to do. The other entity inside of her lingered just under the surface, nearly shimmering like an aura that emanated from her pale, flawless skin. From where I stood, taking another drag of the smoldering cigarette, I could easily feel the ominous energies from that presence residing inside her. I focused on it – until the humanity in me began to pulse and beat against me, thirsting to be set free.

Clearing my throat, I threw the spent cigarette butt on the cement sidewalk and stepped on it, extinguishing any remaining heat as I watched her. Blythe was her name, Blythe McAlister. As she opened the glass doors to the art gallery across the street, I watched eagerly as she disappeared inside.

Seeing her, so normal and superficially carefree, brought everything into focus. She was born into this, the monster inside of her slowly developing and strengthening until it peaked at maturity and surfaced. My own creation was not nearly as gradual, or even graceful. It was terrifying and painful, and lay waste to everything my life had once been.

The images of that horrific night pushed unbidden into my mind, and as I walked away from the gallery – and the beautiful woman – the memory pulled me down into its depths.

The night was far darker than previous ones I could remember.  As I sat outside the home I shared with my beautiful wife Eos, taking in the wonderfully cool night air that brushed my flesh I heard the sounds of the nightlife in the distance. We had planned to start a family, but it was difficult while I lived in the barracks with the other men. Finally, I earned my keep at the age of thirty and became an equal – making it so I could finally wake up to Eos' gorgeous hazel eyes that I was certain any child we bore would inherit.

I looked over the broad expanse of Sparta, the toga I wore light to accommodate for the coolness of the oncoming luke-warm months. It was typical, due to rising insomnia caused by worry, for me to sit outside and marvel at the blinking stars in the night sky.

Something large was just on the horizon.

Shuffling came from behind me, and I turned to see Eos gliding toward me, her long dark hair past her waist – mesmerizingly beautiful and shining in the moonlight that filtered into the small courtyard. Her eyes glimmered, stunning as she watched me carefully when she approached. As I sat, she stood in front of me in her peplos, exposing just enough of her thigh for me to trace my fingers along the bare flesh.

Entwining my fingers delicately in her soft curls, I looked deep into her eyes – worshipping her without saying a single word.

"What woke you, my love? Are you all right?" I enquired, rubbing my thumb along the lock of deep brown hair. "I did not wake you, did I?"

She sighed; her lips parted just slightly with exasperation.

"I'm all right. I am just not feeling well. What are you doing out here, Kallias? You should be resting in preparation for tomorrow evening. Is that what's kept you up?"

As she stared adoringly down at me, I had to tell her the truth under the stars that could never match her beauty.

"You know I would never lie to you. Yes, I am worried. I have no idea what to expect out of this," I paused, trying to find the correct word, "ritual. They are certain it creates much stronger warriors, but I have been told nothing about it."

"Other than that a practitioner has come from Magna Graecia to perform it," she finished.

"Yes," I responded with a slight nod.

Eos reached up gingerly, tracing along my hairline with her fingertips, and then down to my jaw – leading up to my lips. I eagerly kissed them and leaned forward to place my forehead against her belly in surrender – to her and to the sleep I had felt pulling at me since the sun left the sky. It had been at least three nights I had barely slept, the concern over the oncoming ritual playing over and over in my mind.

I felt her hands in my hair, and nearly succumbed to fatigue as I sat there with her. That was, until she spoke again – taking a deep breath that I felt deep within her body. She truly had no idea how much I loved and worshipped her, and now that I had proven myself, I hoped I could do her the honor of giving her children with the time we now got to spend together since I no longer resided in the communal barracks.

"Come to bed with me. I'll help you sleep," she said.

When I looked up at her again, I saw the desire in her eyes, and my own body responded readily to her and the fire inside her. A devious smile played at her lips, and she took my hand in hers – attempting to pull me to my feet so I would follow.

Of course, I went willingly, and I finally slept.

It was night. Everything important and dark seemed to happen at night. The moon hung in the sky and light reflected down on me as I approached the building toward the outskirts. It was the home of this great man that supposedly created stronger soldiers with just one spell – one enchantment. His words seemingly derived directly from the Gods themselves, as I could not understand them. I was willing to do whatever I had to for Sparta. As a soldier, we were conditioned to do so, but even I wondered just how far I was truly willing to go, and how this man would change me. Would it truly be for the better, or for worse?

When I approached the door, Anaxis – another soldier – stood just inside with arms crossed, waiting for my arrival. He had been through this not even six months prior. I had known him before and after – since the age of seven when we began training -- and something had changed in him that I could not quite explain. Except for the change in the hue of his eyes. They used to be a deep, chestnut brown, but changed to an almost glowing, sea-colored blue that left you mesmerized if you stared into them long enough. He was gritty, determined, and wiser beyond his years, but not only that. He was just more. Something lingered just underneath that put my nerves on edge. Something almost… predatory.

He came to attention, straightening his back and pushing away from the wall when I entered. I had been told prior that there was no need for formal introductions. Or knocking for that matter. This man, this magician, had no secrets from what I knew of him.

"Kallias, thank goodness. We thought we lost you." Anaxis gestured toward the back of the small house and down a hallway that led straight into a courtyard half the size of my own. "Please, follow me. You are the only person taking part in the ceremony tonight and he wants to act as quickly as possible before we lose the moon to the clouds."

I followed him quickly, sticking at his back as closely as I could. Despite the size of the home, I did not want to become separated from my friend and comrade. I felt uncomfortable enough, and anxious. The sky opened up above us, and I took a deep breath of the slightly muggy air. It filled my lungs and settled there, taking deep residence that would have felt like drowning if the humidity was any higher.

An older man – long beard peaking past the folds of his cloak – stood in the short distance away on a dais with a small altar in the center. Something the height of a small infant sat on the altar, covered with a heavy cloth that barely hid a soft green glow underneath.

Curiosity piqued, and the closer we came to the figure of the man, my skin buzzed with both apprehension and excitement that sang deep within my very core. It was then that I noticed other robed figures who stood around the platform in a wide circle, hands joined together in reverence. Humming echoed through the empty air, and when we came to the podium, Anaxis dropped to one knee in honor of the man. I remained standing. As a soldier of honor within the ranks of Sparta, I was not about to bow to an unknown whether everyone else did or not. Growing up, I had been known as *resilient*, and the same still rang true into manhood. It had gotten me into some trouble when I was younger, but it helped me in these moments – when met with strange circumstances.

And this was definitely strange.

# ROOTS OF DECEIT   Kindra Sowder

The man in the cloak turned toward us, reaching up to drop his hood around his shoulders. His fingers were slender and gnarled with age, his face echoing the same sentiments of his time on Earth. The wrinkles in his face were heavy, especially along his mouth and forehead, making him look more trodden than any patch of ground. His eyes were dark and sunken, nearly disappearing as he blinked down at Anaxis and myself from the raised platform. The expression on his face revealed weariness as well as well-earned respect.

Leaning down with outstretched arms, he lectured, "Please, Anaxis, that is not necessary. Stand with pride like the Spartan you are. You have been bestowed a gift and you shall not bow down to anyone. Do you understand?"

"Yes, Pythagoras," Anaxis responded, rising to his feet and standing perfectly straight.

Confusion bloomed in my mind and belly at the name. It ran rampant through Greece based on his practices, as well as those of his followers. Extreme as I felt it was, I had also heard of his brilliance when it came to mathematics, but why was he here? The last any had heard, he had been killed in Magna Graecia along with some of his followers – burned alive.

"Forgive me, but the last I heard, you perished. How are you here?" I asked, taking a bold step forward – my tone rather forceful and completely skeptical.

"Or so, they thought." Pythagoras beamed at the mention of his supposed fate, the trickery in his eyes perfectly evident.

"Are you not worried you would be found out? Especially using your given name?" I asked.

"Oh, he is not bothered by such things," Anaxis cut in.

"You're right, Anaxis, I am not bothered by the prospect. I am a practitioner of strong magics, which cloak me from their awareness. Not even the Fates can see or hear of me any longer, not even in name. I possess a power granted by the Underworldly Gods, of which I have bestowed on your brothers – and that you are to receive at the behest of the state."

"Oh?" I said with the curious cocking of one eyebrow.

"Why, yes, Kallias. You are an excellent soldier, but they felt that you could benefit from the ruthless spirit I am about to gift you," he explained.

"And that is?" I probed.

"The spirit of the succubus, dear man." He looked to Anaxis. "Is he always so skeptical?"

Anaxis nodded beside me, "Yes, always."

"Maybe it is because I do not believe in such things," I responded. "The Gods, yes. But a succubus, not in the slightest. No disrespect, of course."

"Of course," Pythagoras mirrored with a curt nod.

A beat of quiet moved through us aside from the humming figures surrounding the dais.

With a deep breath, the older gentleman continued, "Are we ready to begin?"

I hesitated, opened my mouth, and closed it again – really considering his question. I was not a believer in the fantastic beasts, but what if I were wrong? What if this turned me into a dark creature that fed on women? According to what little I had been told, it would only make me stronger, and my observations of Anaxis had said just that. But what if that was not the whole truth? Especially, considering the one physical change I did see. It was small, but who would fail to notice suddenly blue eyes?

"Kallias? Are you ready?" Anaxis asked, irritated concern littering his tone.

Startled, my head swiveled to look at him, and our eyes met. That haunting blue dulled by the moonlight and the torches crept up my spine and wriggled into my brain, but I could not say no, could I?

The simple answer was that I could not, no matter how Anaxis looked at me. No matter how he had changed. The eyes may have been the only physical change from the man I grew up with – trained with – but his personality had shifted as well. Could I take this change, if it did take place, and show it to poor Eos who was so happy to have me in our home? Would I fall out of favor if I walked away? And that was if the state would allow it.

No. I knew better than that. Soldiers, even those in my position, took orders and followed through. Taking part in this ritual was an order.

I nodded and straightened my back while squaring my shoulders. "Yes, I am ready."

Anaxis clapped me on the shoulder and the hit reverberated through my back and chest. Pythagoras seemed pleased, turning back toward the altar while raising his hood back onto his head.

I barely caught a glimpse of the cloth-covered figure before Anaxis pulled my attention again.

He leaned into me, taking my hand in his. It was no secret we were lovers while in the barracks before mine and Eos' marriage, which made the change in him so striking. Eos knew, but she also knew the love in my heart was always meant for her. Clasping my hand tightly, he brought it into his chest and concealed the supportive squeeze with a gruff embrace.

"It will be all right, Kallias," he said.

"I hold no fear," I replied, pulling away far enough so I could see the fine scruff on his jaw.

"I can see the hesitation in your face, brother. I know you."

"I promise, I am not afraid, Anaxis."

He studied me for a moment before glancing back up at the dais. I followed his gaze, and it settled on the sight of the green light coming from underneath the cloth on the altar. Pythagoras stood behind it, hands hovering reverently over the crown of the statue.

"This will change you for the rest of your life, Kallias. I can promise you that."

A deep, dark part of me believed him.

Standing on the dais, facing the moon, I stood as naked as a newborn babe – the slight chill of the air rippling through my body. I shuddered slightly but held strong. Pythagoras stood next to the altar just opposite of where I was, Anaxis having slid a robe over his own body and joined the mass of worshippers around us.

Every color was muted by the darkness – all except for one. I glanced at Pythagoras as he hummed, joining the chorus of the others, a green glow growing brighter and peeking out from underneath the cloth.

Fear took residence in my chest as I listened to their thrumming voices join in with the sounds of nightlife and insects, growing louder in concert as if they knew what was about to take place. I felt like my heart was beating so fast it would find its way into my throat. Swallowing hard, I listened to the sounds as they grew ever louder. The humming turned into a mash of words I did not understand – a language that sounded exotic, and terrifying all at once. It drew me in as I felt warmth begin in the pit of my belly. The rhythm began to pull at my mind, but I shook it away. I wanted to be aware of every moment, no matter what happened.

A soft tingling began in my feet and snaked its way up into the rest of my body at such a pace it almost stole my breath.

I had not been certain of the magic before. I had been skeptical, but now, as I stood here and felt the odd sensations roll through me, I wanted to believe in it more than anything.

Pythagoras' words grew even louder, and then everything ceased – all sound coming to a halt. Even the animals and insects quieted in honor of such a ritual. Reaching out with his right hand, sleeve of the robe brushing the stone of the altar, his fingers took hold of the cloth and yanked it up, dropping it to the altar – figure underneath finally revealed.

I choked out the gasp that threatened to escape. What lie under the soft cloth was a small statue – a bust – of what I assumed was a woman, but this was different. The woman's form was slim, athletic, and seemed to reach out to the Heaven's, crouched down low with arms across her belly. Gray rock covered stone that resembled emerald, but much clearer. It glowed brilliantly, the light it emanated only growing stronger despite the silence as every practitioner around me focused on it. Even the warmth of the low hum inside my body, mind, and chest ceased.

Lightning cracked through the sky from out of nowhere, and the voices rose above the cadence of the rolling wind. Pain. Hot, searing pain shoved itself into my abdomen and lanced out through my entire body – splicing through my veins and each nerve-ending like lightning slashed through me. The scream that built in my chest exploded through my vocal cords with such veracity it was startling.

I was fire – pure, cleansing, and shattering all at once.

The figure of the woman lit up the night from its home on the altar, showing through the small cracks if its rocky shell. The terror I had felt before turned into the most intense wonder and amazement I had ever experienced. My mind was electric, and my heart beat so rapidly in my chest I was certain it would burst from within my ribcage.

All I heard was the roaring wind and the rising voices around me. Then my vision turned brilliant white before every part of my body went numb, my head swam, and then everything went pitch dark.

Everything came back in crystal clear focus, especially the agony of whatever transformation was taking place. My knees gave out completely, causing me to fall onto the hard stone of the dais, scraping both kneecaps. A scream left my mouth unbidden.

Pythagoras came around the dais slowly, approaching me as if he were approaching a wounded predator. He pushed back the hood of his heavy cloak, and his eyes lit up with the emerald energy of the statuette. Then he did something I did not expect him to do. He smiled. Why would he smile while I was in such agony? Tears began to stream down my face, taking every bit of strength I had with them.

"Do not fight it. Let the change take you, Kallias," he encouraged.

It was like those words opened a dam, and I let go of everything, sending everything that flowed through me out into the air and the undulating skies. Thunder rolled and the wind blew, cooling my blazing flesh.

I looked up at the dark clouds above our heads, and blue lightning streaked out from a central point and across the blanket they created. My entire body slackened, and the world quickly fell away. I did not feel the impact of my body hitting the stone.

I barely remembered anything after that, but flashes of images surfaced when I barely woke. I was in my own bed, Eos laying at my side with her body spread out, her beautiful curves beckoning. Blood, deep and warm, began to creep over her bare hip. Shaking my head, I knew it could not be real, but it remained. My eyes stung and exhaustion overtook me again, pulling me down into the deep, crimson-filled depths as image after image of blood, sweat, and screaming mouths forced their way into my dreams – turning them into terrifying nightmares.

Nothing would be the same ever again. I did not need anyone to tell me that. I just knew.

I was dreaming — the only hint provided to me of it being that I stood on the same dais surrounded by nothing. Not even a cloud, or the clatter of thunder and lightning. Complete silence taking me down further into a deep void, like a vacuum.

Heart pounding in my throat, I took a hesitant step forward, just realizing I was completely nude. No toga – no cloak – not even sandals to cover my feet. The stone of the dais was rough against my soles as I stepped forward once more, even closer to the nothing now.

What was this place?

"Hello," I called out helplessly into the void.

No reply. Only the exquisite, deafening quiet answered back. That and my breathing filled whatever kind of space I occupied. A part of me wanted to say it was my mind I stood in, but the rest felt as if I were standing in a physical place. It felt finite and infinite all at once, bringing everything into sharp focus. Even the texture of my skin came to life in brilliant detail.

"Hello," I shouted again. "Is anyone out there?"

Nothing again, but when I turned the missing statuette that had not been there previously, suddenly appeared – glowing brilliant against the blackness.

A shrill, feminine scream shattered the silence into a million pieces. I turned as quickly as I could toward the cry, my body instantly crouching defensively – ready to pounce and to protect. As a Spartan, it was my duty. Another scream tore through the air, and I was caught off-guard by how familiar it sounded. When my eyes caught sight of two figures before me, I froze in pure shock at the sight of so much red. A man, large and intimidating, crouched over a soft yielding woman.

Eos.

Blood poured from the center of her chest; her gorgeous eyes dead as they stared up at me from the absent ground while her blood soaked into the startlingly white peplos she wore.

"No," I growled, turning into a primal yell.

Pouncing from the dais, my feet somehow connected with the ground that did not exist, and I reached out toward the man harming my beautiful Eos. My fingers dug into the man's muscular shoulder and forced him up to face me. When he came to stand erect, my own face stared back at me, and the terror I had felt to begin with replaced the need to protect. His eyes were wide, jaw clenched as he took me in – enraged by my interference.

Then I saw recognition in his eyes – the deep brown eyes that mirrored mine – and a sinister smirk took residence on his mouth. It took that moment for me to realize that Eos' blood, bright red against his tanned skin, coated his lips and ran down his chin. Almost like he had been tasting her, but I was too scared to look down at her lifeless form.

"What have you done?" I screamed.

The grin on my face only grew wider as he stared back at me, a large, thick droplet of blood running down the bottom lip that mirrored my own. I felt my chin quiver, but still refused to look at Eos. She had not moved since I jerked the fiend away from her, which caused my heart to grow still in my chest with fear. The figure stood tall and strong, large muscles flexing as we circled one another like animals would in the wild.

# ROOTS OF DECEIT   KINDRA SOWDER

"Oh, what have I done?" the man asked in my own voice, using my own mouth and throat to form the words. "What have you done?"

My foot brushed a soft lock of hair, and then flesh that has already begun to cool. I could not stop myself. I looked down at what used to be my beautiful wife who had been replaced with a corpse – her mouth hung wide open as she lay on her back, blood flowing from her open lips. Her eyes were nearly bulging from their sockets in terror, but I could not tear my eyes from the most glaring imperfection of them all. Fresh, glistening meat watched my every move from the gaping hole in her chest – heart missing where she had held it for me for at least a decade. Shock and bewilderment tore through my insides, immediately met with grief and absolute horror at what the other me had done. What *I* had done.

I was too startled to move. I did not dare hold her again for fear of tearing apart her beautiful visage any more than had already been accomplished. Her chilling flesh against my own warm skin was enough to stop me cold.

"This was not me," I whispered, more to myself than the mirror image of me standing there watching covered in crimson.

It ran down his chest and down to his thighs. I wanted to run from the vision, but I knew I could not. I was trapped in my own mind – in the nightmare I felt I could never wake from. A chill ran down my spine and settled in the base of my soul, turning it black and dead.

"This was not me. You did this," I yelled, pointing at my own image standing in front of me.

He shook his head. "But you wanted this, Kallias. You thirst for blood and for violence. I see it in your mind and your heart. You cannot hide that from me because I am you. I am a part of you that you can no longer escape from no matter how hard you try. It is the reason you did not walk away from the ritual. You wanted to be free from the confines of your morality, and now... you can be."

"What are you?" I asked, my voice so much smaller than it had been previously.

The man that looked just like me laughed, loud and boisterous – so much like myself when I allowed an unhindered performance, which was typically only with Eos. The smirk that replaced the uproarious, bolstering laughter was horrifying, causing terror to rip through me like a torrent. We continued to circle one another, but then he stopped, and I stopped with him –

with myself. We moved like a singular unit now, but it seemed unnatural.

"I know you feel it, Kallias. You feel it in your bones. *I* am *you*. We are one in every way – mind, body, and soul. I am the succubus. I now reside in your muscles and your bones. *You* are *me*. *I* am *you*. We are *one*."

My head shook without my permission. "No, I am not like you."

"You are not like me, you fool. You are me. If you do not accept this, your transformation will be most painful." My visage paused thoughtfully, and then spoke again. "Would you want to leave your beautiful Eos to fend for herself? For another soldier to replace you in her bed? Anaxis, perhaps?"

The image of my friend and old lover flashed into my mind, his bright blue eyes taking over everything against his tanned flesh. Shaking the image away, I beat the side of my head with my open palm, refusing to let this creature beat me into submission with horrid thoughts. Anaxis would never betray me in such a fashion. We were brothers now, and our bond was as strong as an ox. Possibly even stronger. But could it be overpowered by my resistance? Could he steal my powerful, beautiful Eos from me because I chose to struggle?

Could I take the risk?

My heart lurched in my chest and my stomach churned at the thought of leaving my wonderful wife to her own devices. How would she fair with the brutal Anaxis? Was this creature – the succubus – right?

"I see the fear in you, soldier. You know I am right. I will make you stronger as the old man promised, and you can hold onto your Eos," he cooed.

"What do I do?" I asked out of the same fear he saw in me – weakness, which I had never shown before. "How do I gain your strength?"

A smile crept onto his face, and his body smoothed out into a much less defensive posture. His shoulders relaxed and his arms slackened, almost as if he had expected me to attack. That would not be the case. I was weak, and the thought of leaving Eos in the hands of a fate without me ate at my mind and my heart.

"You must accept me into every part of you. Let me fill you and your existence, and you will have all that you desire," he said. "Can you accept me, Kallias?"

"Yes, I can," I breathed, the enormity of what I was saying barreling into me.

# ROOTS OF DECEIT  Kindra Sowder

Moving forward, he put his arms out toward me as if to embrace me and stepped into my chest. Face-to-face, I could see the crimson blood drying on his lips and down his chin and chest, but I did not flinch away. I remained, ready to accept him – myself – in whatever way was necessary.

"Embrace me, Kallias. Accept me," he whispered.

I did as requested, wrapping my arms around myself with my heart hammering inside my chest. Closing my eyes, I felt warmth begin in my belly, rumbling and spreading outward from my navel. As it spread, I felt acceptance and calmness wash over me.

I awoke to the feel of our bed, cool and comforting against my skin that was far too warm. Light filtered in from outside. I felt as normal as could be expected except for the solid pit of heat in my belly that seemed to live there now. Sitting up, I stretched out my stiff muscles, seeing that I was indeed naked like I had been in my dream. Eos' beautiful soprano singing voice floated in through the threshold. My ears pricked at the sound, and I turned my head to hear the sounds of moving of bowls and other things that hinted at the first meal of the day being set. Her voice was like a song, and I closed my eyes, taking the deepest of breaths my lungs could hold as if taking her into me as well.

Then I felt it.

The squirm of energy inside me, the pit just inside stretching out and spreading like a living thing. My mind went back into the dream, realizing the sensation felt familiar. When the succubus had asked for acceptance, it was real. The succubus had to live inside me now. I knew it despite having never believed in it before. Placing my palm against my stomach, it squirmed even more, and there was a ping in my head that I shook away – trying to remain myself even with the invading presence.

Swallowing, I tried my best to ignore it, and stood up – reaching out to pick up my toga and shuffle into it so I was decent enough just in case. Walking out into the open space of our home, I was greeted with an amazing sight. Eos fussed over a table filled with some of the most extravagant fair we had ever had in our home. Typically, we would feast on tagenias and olives, but there was so much more before me than usual. The tagenias were still there, but there were also figs and other fruits as well as wine and breads.

# ROOTS OF DECEIT  Kindra Sowder

"Good morning, my love," I said, stopping just behind her as she busied herself placing a bowl of halved figs on the table.

I wrapped my arms around her, and she turned to face me, her eyes and face alight with a glow I had never seen in her before.

"Good morning," she breathed, her breath sweet like the figs.

She placed a soft, loving kiss on my lips.

"You seem very happy today," I said. "And this is quite the feast. Are you celebrating something?"

"We are," she said, reaching behind her to pluck a fig from the table.

She placed it at my lips, the light in her eyes never extinguishing, and I opened it to take the deliciously sweet fruit into my mouth. The flavor coated my tongue, and as I swallowed, I twirled my fingers through the soft ringlets of her deep chestnut hair. The presence inside me continued to spread out through my muscles, but I ignored it as best as I could. My lovely Eos was always of the utmost importance.

"I saw the physician while you were sleeping before I went to the market."

"Are you all right? Are you ill?"

She shook her head with the smile still on her face. "No, I am not ill." She paused, seeming to think something over before parting her luscious lips. "I am with child."

"By the Gods, are you sure?" I asked, the smile taking control of my mouth before I could stop it.

"Yes, my love, I am sure."

Her smile was bright and wide, reaching her eyes and making them glitter with happiness. Joy and excitement caused my heart to race faster than if I were in battle, battling with my urge to slow its frantic beating.

Sinking to my knees, I rested my palms on her flat belly, wishing to speak with the life growing just within her flesh. The life we had created almost stole all breath from my lungs, my breathes hard and fast.

"Are you happy?" she questioned, looking down at me while running her fingers through my hair.

Not looking away from our child's resting place, I replied with a gracious laugh, "Yes, my beautiful Eos. I am happy beyond words." I planted a gentle kiss just below her navel and turned to lay my head against her softness. "You, my little one, will be the pride of the Gods."

Eos' hands continued to rake gently through my hair – lovingly.

"Now, don't put too much pressure on our unborn child, Kallias. Maybe he or she will only seek to bring pride to you as their father," she said.

"Ah," I chuckled, "I suppose that would be all right, then."

Stroking the most tender part of her belly with my thumb, I felt something swell inside my chest. Pride, joy, and anticipation resided there, but something else stirred within. The thought of the presence of the spirit Pythagoras brought to life within me flashed through my mind, bringing a twinge of fear in my chest with it. It almost felt like my heart gave a lurch, and then each valve clamped down and refused to let blood flow in and out in perfect rhythm. The shock of recognition ceased its movement for all of a moment, growing stronger as I remained with my cheek pressed against Eos, listening for the life germinating inside her – despite knowing I would not be able to hear it or feel it just yet.

I closed my eyes and kneeled there before her as I silently worshipped her and attempted to dampen the rising presence that threatened to choke me. Gripping her, I just breathed and listened to the hushed sounds of our home and her body. The presence stirred and shifted deep in my belly, attempting to spread out through my entire body as I kneeled there and held onto whatever sanity remained. It was an odd sensation, kind of like something slithering through my intestines and winding through each and every organ. At first, it was almost imperceptible, but quickly grew in intensity – the harder I attempted to hold it at bay, the harder it fought against me. Of course, I was not certain what the result would be if I were to let it take over. A part of me was too afraid to allow it.

"Please, Kallias, stand and come eat with me. I bought all of this from the market to celebrate," Eos said.

Turning my face up toward her voice, I opened my eyes. The sight of her was breathtaking as always. Her long brown hair flowed down in soft curls and her eyes were alight with glee that penetrated the new darkness I felt.

"Can I just stay down here and thank the Gods for the generous gift they have granted us?" I asked, rubbing my palms on her stomach.

She laughed a rich, hearty laugh, throwing her head back slightly before looking back down at me – smile so wide I envisioned her face cracking in half. I blinked the image away, seeing only her beautiful face unmarred again.

"Not unless you want to feast on the floor."

"I am not against that thought in the slightest."

I reached up, grabbed her arms gently, and quickly pulled her down onto the hard stone floor with me – coming to hover over her. She let out a startled and excited yelp, but did not stop me, laughing all the way down until our eyes met.

"My love, you have blessed me."

She did not say anything, only smiled wider. No words would have done the light in her eyes any justice. The spirit of the succubus stirred inside me again, but I ignored it, kissing her hungrily. It was not long before I was completely short of breath, the desire for my wife flowed through my entire body like a hot tidal wave.

"Kallias," a deep, bass voice much like my own whispered to me in the darkness of slumber, pulling me from a dream I could not remember.

"Kallias."

# ROOTS OF DECEIT  Kindra Sowder

It was the same animalistic version of my own voice I had heard when the succubus first introduced itself to me – frightening and visceral. Demonic. Something I had not believed in before that was more real than ever now when faced with it.

The air left my lungs as if an invisible force had sucked it out, and I awoke, shooting up to a sitting position in bed and gasping. Heart pounding, blood rushed in my ears and my temples thronged, every muscle in my body screaming to run away from the presence taking over. It felt hot in the center of my belly, spreading outward through every part of me that it had not touched yet.

My eyes scanned the room, landing on Eos' prone form in our bed beside me, thin sheet draped over the beautiful curve of her hips – face serene with closed eyes and soft breathing. She was so peaceful, a stark contrast for the battle inside me.

I turned away from her, the sight of her naked body causing the presence to grow into a stronger force. I closed my eyes and took a deep breath as I sat on the edge of our bed, hands gripping it tightly, knuckles white and arms trembling. The presence felt viciously angry and hungry for violence. So hungry for it beyond anything I had ever felt in battle as if it would take anything it could just to see spilled blood.

My leg jumped involuntarily, my heel tapping on the floor in a quick, steady rhythm. But I could not stop it, just like I could not stop the transformation continuing to take place despite my fight against it. Of course, even though I was not certain what this change would do to me, I did know that feeling was unsettling enough for fear to pierce my heart. Heat continued to pour through every part of my body, and swiftly, an odd sensation took over. I felt as if I were being pushed into the background of my mind, while something else was pushing forward to overpower me entirely. The edges of my vision became fuzzy and everything blurred like I was looking out through a gossamer curtain. Anxiety spiked, and a cold sweat broke out over my skin as the heat continued to pour through me like a dam had been left wide open.

The sound of shifting fabric came from behind me, signaling Eos was awake. Had I awoken her? Could she tell something was changing in me? I could not see a physical change in my body, but was there something else?

# ROOTS OF DECEIT  KINDRA SOWDER

I felt her fingers lightly touch my shoulder, then her warm body pressed against me – her breath hot on my neck.

"Kallias? Are you all right? You feel feverish," she asked, placing her palm against my cheek.

The succubus stirred even more, spreading out even quicker as it pushed my own presence even further into the background. My flesh felt warm, fuzzy, and tingly. Sweat beaded on my forehead and upper lip. I felt a small voice in my mind, whispering my name again.

"Kallias, there is no use in fighting me. You accepted me. Now you must accept what I do. Resistance is useless," it purred.

Just like that, something snapped inside me, pushing me so far down into the darkness I could only see what my body did, but could not affect it. No matter how strong my will. It was as if I could only see from the bottom of a deep pit. I could still feel my body move, and the succubus' presence coiled there with me like a snake while using my body to strike.

Pounding against it, I cried out and screamed like a wild animal. I feared what this new presence would do to my beautiful Eos, but the only response to my terror was the succubus' horrifying laughter in the space around me.

"I am fine, my love," I heard and felt myself say, turning to face her while cupping her check with our shared hand. "I am perfect."

It slid down to her slender throat, tracing her collar bones with light fingertips. Every instinct told me to fight, but I was beginning to see that the succubus was right. I could not resist and any urge it had would come to fruition no matter how loud I felt I was screaming. Fear and anguish lanced through me, and I knew that the spirit felt it because it chuckled in our shared mind, and almost purred in response to Eos as she placed her hand on mine. She was like a moth to a flame – easy prey. She always submitted to me as I did to her so our love for each other was never in doubt.

Her eyes met mine, and she smiled playfully, her naked body leaning toward me as my hand continued to stroke her flesh.

"Is this your way of asking for more, my love? Because I will gladly give it," she said through obviously aroused, ragged breaths.

The succubus did not respond – only leaned forward, pressing against her to guide her back down to the bed where it positioned my body above her. My hand – our hand – moved up the length of her body to cup her neck, hungrily kissing her. At first, I thought maybe this would be the extent of the succubus' plans, but I quickly realized I was mistaken when my large hands reached up without my permission, and wrapped around her throat, squeezing tightly.

Her body stiffened, unsure at first, and then she stopped kissing me and attempted to push me off her. My shared eyes looked into hers, and I saw the terror and confusion that lay within. Her fingers clawed at my hands and her legs – wrapped around me – tried to come around to kick at me, but I was much too strong for her. A lot stronger than I had been before the transformation. Tears erupted and then spilled over her lids as she fought with all her tiny body's might against the succubus that had taken over. Crying out inside, I knew she could not hear my grief and apologies for what I had done. The spirit Pythagoras placed inside me, what the state believed would make me a stronger warrior, turned me into something that my poor Eos would fall victim to. I fought, trying push my way out of the well of darkness that enveloped me to no avail.

It was that moment I wished I could explain somehow. That I could tell her I did not wish her dead. That I wanted our child to blossom inside her, and to grow into the Spartan the Gods would be proud of. Then anger at the Gods took over, driving the force of the succubus even further as Eos weakened and the light began to fade from her eyes.

Within mere moments, she ceased to fight, and there was a strange pride that bloomed in my chest alongside my grief that cracked the dark like lightning.

What the creature inside me did next shook me to my very core.

Letting go of her slender throat, bruises littering her pale flesh, it clenched one of my hands into large fists and brought it down hard into the center of her chest. A loud crack filled the air, resonating in my ears as I watched on – horrified. It beat on the same spot again and again until flesh and bone gave way, blood flowing freely past my own fingers as the succubus reached down and pulled pieces of Eos' chest away – her heart, still and crimson, exposed for the world to see. My hand, our hand, reached inside and gripped the organ. Her chest cavity was warm and slick, almost as if she were still alive and breathing, and the muscles of her heart were smooth past the rigid sharp bone that once protected it from harm.

The succubus pulled it out, roughly severing every connection within her body with sheer force, and then brought it up to my lips.

I gagged and begged the creature to stop, but it did not hear me. That, or it ignored my presence completely, reveling in what I thought it was about to make me do. Lips grazed the meat of Eos' heart, and I gagged again, feeling the nausea burn its way into my throat – but it did not seem to affect the spirit. Absolute horror, grief, and disgust spiraled in my mind along with the pride and hunger from the succubus that threatened to take me over completely. It tried to wash me away with Eos' blood but had not succeeded. Not yet.

But still enough.

My lips clung to the organ, and then my teeth bit into its tough exterior. The taste of iron flooded my mouth, coating my tongue in its heat. I felt my stomach heave, and I wanted to vomit, but I could not. I could not ingest the heart Eos had given me. Not like this. Not like a rabid carnivore with no sense of love or loyalty to its partner. The succubus was an animal, that much was clear.

"Kallias," I heard a strong, male voice echo through the room.

It was as if I slammed back into my own body, everything coming into crystal clear focus once again as control came back to me. Horrified, I looked down at what I had been forced to do, and a harsh wail left my throat to meet whoever had said my name.

Anaxis moved from within the shadowed doorway, the magician Pythagoras at his heels.

"What have I done?!" I screamed out, tears like liquid fire streaming down my cheeks.

I dropped the organ to the bed, watching it roll a couple inches and stop nestled in its original resting place – bite marks in it. Heart hammering in my chest and my entire body nearly collapsing with trembling horror, it took a moment for someone to speak. Some sort of shock had registered on their faces first, but then a sly grin plastered itself on Anaxis' face while Pythagoras only nodded in acknowledgement.

"You have made your first kill," Anaxis said – almost whispered.

"What? What is that supposed to mean?" I shrieked, rising from the bed.

Pythagoras took a step forward, moving Anaxis to the side in a rushed manner. "Did you accept the spirit, soldier? Did the succubus come to you?"

I thought about that for a moment, everything a blur over the last hours since the ritual took place. I remembered the important things – Eos telling me she was with child and making love. That was all I could recall.

Then it hit me like fist to the gut, and I almost crumbled to my knees and cried out. The dream. The image of myself that I spoke to that asked me to accept it so I could gain its power and strength. That was it, wasn't it? That was the moment that truly changed everything. My knees nearly buckled, but I held myself up, not willing to give into weakness in front of Anaxis. I could have cared less about the magician.

"Yes." The word barely left my lips. "Yes."

Pythagoras came to the edge of the bed, long robe moving around him as if it had a mind of its own, and looked down sadly as Eos' body – taking in the bloody scene before him. When he looked back up at me, his eyes were still full of the same sorrow, but nothing could compare to the disgust and grief I felt within myself at that moment.

"That was the spirit of the succubus. This," he motioned toward Eos, "is what it does. It kills indiscriminately. It feels no love no matter how much its human shell may contest it. And that is all you are to it now. You are a vessel for murder, Kallias."

"It made me kill my wife," I shouted, my tears mixing with Eos blood all over my face, neck, and chest – running down my legs toward the floor. "She is with child. My wife and child are dead!" Without even thinking, I vaulted over the bed and grabbed the magician by his cloak, pushing him up against the wall in an enraged frenzy. "You did this. What this thing is, you can take it back! Send it back where it came from!" I yelled into his face.

He remained calm, never once showing fear, and placed his old, leathered hands on mine. "I am afraid I cannot do that."

"And why is that? You placed this spirit within me. Surely you can remove it."

"Because it is a part of you now, and will be as long as you live, brother," Anaxis said from behind me, his hands coming to rest on my shoulders.

I jerked away from them both, nearly toppling to the floor in shock.

"Do not touch me. You should have warned me. You are just as bad as the State. I am not some soldier that can be experimented on," I shouted. "The both of you are bastards. How could the Gods allow this?"

"It is your fate. Not even the Gods can stop fate, Kallias," Pythagoras muttered.

Falling to my knees, I looked up at the old magician and sneered. "And what do you know of fate?"

"What I do know is that fate is a cruel mistress, and this was chosen for you before your birth," he replied.

"Nothing can be changed now. You have no choice but to accept your new future," he paused, "without Eos. This journey is meant to be a lonely one, my friend." He kneeled beside me and clapped me on the shoulder.

"I will not love without her, you understand. I cannot, especially knowing my own hands took her life and that of our unborn child."

I lifted my hands, the crimson on my flesh stark in contrast. Almost as if it were mocking me.

"You do not have a choice, soldier," Pythagoras stated. "The succubus will not allow you to die. You are immortal now."

The thought of living life like this, with no control over the murderous urge I felt rising up in me again. I saw Eos' beautiful visage in my mind, smiling up at me as we wed, and my heart ached. The presence rolled in my belly like fire, spreading out into each muscle and nerve fiber with my rage. I felt the same sensations again – my essence being pulled into the darkness.

"No," I hissed to the succubus. "No. Not again."

I fought against *It*, but just as before, resistance was futile. I could not stop the wave that crashed over me.

"Do not fight it, brother. Accept it," Anaxis said, placing a large hand on my back.

Just like that, it was as if everything snapped into place, and I was no longer in control. Everything had changed forever, and there was no going back. The succubus and I were one.

The acrid smell of blood tickled my nostrils, pulling my thoughts from the past and back to my latest kill spread out in front of me. It was as if the time outside watching the artist and then the kill passed in a flash, but I knew better. Images of her cries and body being ripped to ribbons slashed through me, making my heart ache – making Emmet's heart ache. The heart was not mine. Just the body and the mind.

# ROOTS OF DECEIT  Kindra Sowder

Over the centuries, I – the succubus – had held onto control of this form. Kallias has bounced from one identity to another, settling on Emmett Adler while, in this modern time, I became Adam Burnside. Emmett was an artist, and I was his *benefactor*. And that was where all difference ceased to exist

Well, almost.

We later learned that this affliction was not truly supernatural, but the result of radiation morphing the original body's DNA – creating a new person inside the other. One with a murderous rage it could not help, and that every person who became either like we did or by hereditary misfortune could not overcome.

The reason for that, I could not tell, but it existed. It was uncontrollable, that thirst. Not even the blood of a million women could quench it, and now Blythe had caught my interest. The fact that she could nearly coexist with her other half was fascinating, and I needed her secret if I were going to continue on like this for what remained of eternity.

Standing before the body held up by chains on the large metal 'X,' I pushed her bloodied blonde hair away from what used to be a beautiful face. She yawned back at me, sightless since I had removed both blue orbs and devoured them. Her pale skin was blotchy, lips turning blue rather quickly after her death.

Not long after that, I had cracked her rib cage open, reached inside, and pulled out her beating heart as her screams silenced instantly. I had felt Emmett – Kallias – stir inside with disgust when I got down and devoured her heart as well. It was tough and the taste of iron had filled my mouth, still lingering as I stood there.

Reaching up, my fingertips grazed each protruding rib bone that glinted in the dim light. My stomach lurched, and I fought back the vomit that threatened to spill past my lips. Emmett's involuntary reaction to my actions.

I thought of the redhead again.

Blythe McAlister.

What a strange creature she was. It made me wonder – even more so than before – what secrets lie within her mind and body. What could I learn from the differences I had only sensed in her? What was different? What could I use?

What secrets could her particular brand of the same affliction tell me? There was only one way to find out.

# ROOTS OF DECEIT  Kindra Sowder

BLYTHE and Hyde

will return soon

# ABOUT THE AUTHOR

KINDRA SOWDER is from California but currently resides in South Carolina with her author/poet husband, Ed. She also shares her home with two elderly rescue cats that try ridiculously hard to interrupt her thoughts on her next book. Kindra has a MA in English Literature with a minor in Creative Writing specializing in fiction, and a BA in Criminal Neuropsychology. All of which she graduated at the top of her classes. Her greatest achievement is her son, Dechlin.

Keep up with Kindra on Facebook, Snapchat, Twitter, Instagram, TikTok, and her Amazon page.

All of her books are available in Audio, eBook, and Printed versions on Amazon, and wherever fine books are sold. If you do not see it, ask for it.

# ROOTS OF DECEIT  Kindra Sowder

# Also, by KINDRA SOWDER

**THE EXECUTIONER TRILOGY** (re-releasing soon)
> Follow the Ashes
> Follow the Screams
> Follow the Bloodshed

**THE PERMUTATION ARCHIVES**
> The Harvested
> The Pursuit
> The Scorned
> The Defied
> The Clash

**THE INITIATIVE** (re-releasing soon)

> Chasing Shadows

**THE MISS HYDE COLLECTION**
> A Bloody Heritage
> Roots of Deceit
> *An upcoming untitled volume 3*

**THE HEADHUNTER SERIES** w/ Santiago Cirilo
> Zombified
> Resurrection *(Coming February 2023)*

**THE JOHN BAKER CHRONICLES** w/ Bryan Tann
> Invincible Heart
> Unbreakable Mind

**VINDICTA** w/ P. Mattern

## ROOTS OF DECEIT  KINDRA SOWDER

UNDER HELL'S WATCHFUL EYE

(Flash fiction)

THE DELIVERANCE OF DESIREE TANNER

(Flash Fiction)

AND MANY MORE . . .